Killing Violets

(Gods' Dogs)

Killing Violets

(Gods' Dogs)

Tanith Lee

Stafford England

Killing Violets (Gods' Dogs)
By Tanith Lee
© 2012

Cover by John Kaiine
Layout by Storm Constantine

Set in Palatino Linotype

ISBN 978-1-907737-36-7

IP0108

Author Web Site: http://www.tanith-lee.com

An Immanion Press Edition
8 Rowley Grove
Stafford ST17 9BJ
http://www.immanion–press.com
info@immanion–press.com

A Selection from her 93 titles

The Birthgrave Trilogy (The Birthgrave; Vazkor, son of Vazkor,
Quest for the White Witch)
The Vis Trilogy (The Storm Lord; Anackire; The White Serpent)
The Flat Earth Opus (Night's Master; Death's Master; Delusion's
Master; Delirium's Mistress; Night's Sorceries)
Don't Bite the Sun
Drinking Sapphire Wine
The Paradys Quartet (The Book of the Damned; The Book of the
Beast; The Book of the Dead; The Book of the Mad)
The Venus Quartet (Faces Under Water; Saint Fire; A Bed of Earth;
Venus Preserved)
Sung in Shadow
A Heroine of the World
The Scarabae Blood Opera (Dark Dance; Personal Darkness;
Darkness, I)
The Blood of Roses
When the Lights Go Out
Heart-Beast
Elephantasm
Reigning Cats and Dogs
The Unicorn Trilogy (Black Unicorn; Gold Unicorn; Red Unicorn)
The Claidi Journals (Law of the Wolf Tower; Wolf Star Rise, Queen
of the Wolves, Wolf Wing)
The Piratica Novels (Piratica 1; Piratica 2; Piratica 3)
The Silver Metal Lover
Metallic Love
The Gods Are Thirsty

Collections

Nightshades
Dreams of Dark and Light
Red As Blood – Tales From the Sisters Grimmer
Tamastara, or the Indian Nights
The Gorgon
Tempting the Gods
Hunting the Shadows
Sounds and Furies

Also Published by Immanion Press

The Colouring Book Series

Greyglass
To Indigo
L'Amber

Contents

Who has never loved has never lived. Or died.

To Begin

In the European city where he found her, Anna had already made up her mind to sell herself. She was very hungry. She had begun to hallucinate about food. But something had decided Anna's body was worth more than a dinner. What it was worth is the substance of this story.

Raoul met her by the banks of the pea-green river, to which she had wandered down. Around them the grey city rose through a grey rain, with one or two buildings like parma ham, while some copper domes shone like spectral turnips. Old woodsmoke burning somewhere had the smell of chocolate.

When Anna turned, her large rain-coloured eyes fixed at once on Raoul. She saw he was well-dressed, and he was smoking too, an expensive cigarette. That he was handsome made her think she should be careful. Surely he had no reason to be looking, with his black eyes, for a street girl.

"Good day. Do you like the rain?" said Raoul.

"What rain?" said Anna. It had tasted of thin French wine.

"This one, which falls on the just and the unjust together."

"Which are you?" asked Anna.

He laughed. What lovely teeth. "I see you're a

foreigner, like myself. Rain falls on foreigners, too. I'd like to take you somewhere."

Anna felt a surge of hope so painful she nearly screamed. "Oh, where?" she said, negligently, watching some ducks go by. But they did not look like food in their feathers, and now she could smell brown soup from the river mud.

"To my hotel, perhaps?" said Raoul.

So he *was* looking for a street girl. And she must be his type, slim and ash-coloured, and belted into a poor coat, whose pockets held all she owned, water dripping from the sides of her bell-shaped hat, and from the wisps of her short hair.

"Why would I go with you?" said Anna, seeing the clouds above the rain, marshmallow, or scoops of soiled creamed potato.

"We could have some dinner, some drinks. We'd have a nice time," he said. Then he added, strangely she thought, possibly sinisterly, "I don't have odd tastes. I'd like to fuck you, but there won't be anything - unnatural."

Anna said, "Let's, then."

She walked arm in arm with him - he had gallantly offered his arm.

The puddles sang at her high heels and splashed her legs, her last pair of stockings.

She had absolutely no thoughts at all about the love-making. She would do whatever he wanted, even squat on the rug giving grunts like a pig. She began to float, weightlessly, nearly floating right away from him, so it was a good thing she had his arm to cling to.

No one looked askance in the lobby of the hotel, which was one of the grand stone piles of the city, lined with awful maroon carpets several inches thick, marble stairs and pillars, pale green walls that reminded her of celery.

Even so, they dined in his room. Of course, she wasn't fit for the gilded dining apartment.

His suite was lavish and grotesque, with a chandelier. He asked if she would like a cocktail. She said she would. The drink came in grey-rain glasses, with olives and caviar and toast, and Anna ate. She ate, she ate.

As she ate the meal - she was never able afterwards to remember what it was, only the caviar and the cocktail at the beginning - pickles and patés and the entrée and a dessert and fruit - she kept thinking fondly, nearly enthusiastically, that she would do anything, anything for him. All he wished. Tie him to the bed-posts and bite his toes, beat him with the fire-tongs, pretend to be dead...

But she had eaten nothing, before this dinner, for five days, and drunk only two cups of coffee. Ten minutes after she had set down the last spoon or knife, she wobbled into his bathroom of mahogany and brass, and vomited copiously and ceaselessly for nearly two hours.

Finally she found herself lying, damp and shivering, and only semi-conscious, tucked into the luxurious bed. A hot stone water-bottle was being placed at her feet by a faceless female hotel attendant, and Raoul was wringing out a cloth in ice-water for her head.

Presently, when they were again alone, "I'm sorry," said Anna, the first words she had been able to speak for some while. "How disgusting. How *ungrateful*."

Raoul sat looking at her. As his splendid dark-browed face came back into focus, she saw only an amused sympathy on it. This gave her, and was to continue to give her for some time, an elevated idea of Raoul, his philosophies and wisdoms, his tolerance of life and of her.

"You should have told me," said Raoul, "that you were actually in a starved condition."

"I was only greedy, and stupid," she murmured. And fell asleep.

If she had thought about it, which she had had no time to do, she would have imagined he would be going to bundle her out in the morning, perhaps with a few banknotes, maybe only with a disagreeable curse.

In fact, when she woke he was gone, leaving her a note. The note told her to do as she wished in the suite; he had ordered her a very light meal. She must relax. He would see her that evening.

Anna sat in the bed, eating the hot roll and drinking the milk. Then she got up and had a long, scented bath in the enormous marble tub.

When Raoul returned, she was lying asleep again in the bed. She was naked, and had been waiting, to make things up to him.

But cheerfully he only told her, if she was strong enough, to get up. He had hired a gown for her. They would dine downstairs.

A woman came and did Anna's hair and nails. There was powder, lipstick, and more scent. Lingerie and stockings. The gown was beaded grey silk. More rain. It suited her.

At first, going into the dining-room, seeing all the guests, the straight-laced little orchestra, the palms, and candles burning, and again smelling the food, she felt faint.

But Raoul guided her to a table. She ate sensibly now, and only a little. She drank two glasses of the red wine to please him, because he insisted it would strengthen her.

Then she felt like crying for a moment, because he had been so kind, because she had never thought she would ever sit in such a place again. Or rather, not for many years, perhaps not until she was middle-aged, or old.

At last, she diffidently touched his hand.

"Shall we go upstairs?" she timidly asked. She was becoming desperate to thank him, to pay him. To have it over and face grim reality once more. She had proved extremely costly.

"Yes, in a minute. But I want to ask you something, Anna."

"Yes, Raoul."

"Do you believe in love at first sight?"

Anna frowned. She had not expected this; it was like speaking of fairies or ghosts, probably speaking of them in the middle of a violent storm at sea or when hanging off a wire in mid-air.

"I don't know."

"I didn't either," said Raoul. "I don't even know if I do now. But something - something has happened."

Abruptly, she realized he meant himself, and her. Before she could stop it she giggled. How awful. Quickly she said, "I'm sorry. The wine, it's made me silly..."

"That's all right, Anna. This must seem extraordinary. But there you are. I might have taken it more slowly, but I have to go back tonight. Start back. I mean, back to England."

A wave of relief rushed over her and through her blood and heart. He must be one of those men who preferred to pretend love when they made it. But then, he had been so direct by the river. He had used, then, only the positive word, *fuck*.

"Anna," he said, "I have to be at the station in an

hour. And I want you to come with me."

"Of course I will." There was no time, evidently, even for sex. She would offer it, of course. A quick rough fling.

"You don't understand," he said calmly. "I want you to get on the train with me. To travel with me."

"Where?" One of her first questions, repeated.

"To England, Anna. Oh, it sounds preposterous. But you're lost here, aren't you? You've no one and nothing. I don't want to intrude. I won't ask you anything. We know nothing about each other, do we? Isn't that rather wonderful? Like two books bound with skin. We can read each other as we go. Or not. Frankly I don't care if you never tell me anything. Just - *be* with me."

He was not pleading. He didn't sound desperate or unbalanced. It occurred to her he might lead her on to the phantasmal train, carry her away over the map of Europe, and in some dark forest, as the train roared on, slice her throat or hang her from a pine.

You met a wet girl in the rain. You took her to your hotel and fed her and heard her throwing up for hours, and from this you *loved* her? You *wanted* her? He looked self-possessed, beautiful, rich, and utterly certain.

"I don't..." she said softly.

"I'm afraid it has to be yes or no. The trains are all over the place - I thought I had until midnight to talk you round. I've bought a ticket for you. I've got a sleeper. It won't be uncomfortable. I'll take care of you, Anna. Wouldn't that be a relief, after what you've had to put up with?"

"Oh, it wasn't much," she said. She lowered her eyes. "You've been wonderfully kind. But..."

"Yes or no, Anna. Say it now."

"But I can't - I can't - it isn't..." she said wildly. "I

may disappoint you..."

"Sexually, you mean?"

"Yes, and in all ways."

He laughed. Like before.

Then he took her hand, and squeezed it. And his clasp was warm and strong.

To ourselves, we are the centre of the universe. How can it be otherwise? Dissemble to ourselves and others all we may, it is not ultimately incredible to us that we should be recognised, by the gods.

When they got up, it was with an accomplished ease that she glided before him from the dining-room.

And in the smart travelling clothes he had bought her - just her size, as the gown had been - she next proceeded him to the taxi.

The station loomed in blocks of smoke and steam, the lights flickering, roars of motion and agitation everywhere. But they were led, by uniformed men, to their secure compartment.

Exhaustion felled her. She sat on the lower bunk. Raoul kissed her hand.

"Sleep, Anna. There's no hurry, now."

He did not make love to her until the second night.

Dizzy with wine and the motion of the train, she lay with her arms outflung, her legs lifted so the tender backs of her knees were on his shoulders.

His kisses shivered like feathers into her sexual core. As he stroked her breasts she forgot everything, her past, her future. Harp glissandi, sensations of fizzing, and sweet ache. She seized his shoulders frantically. The train bounced her up and down and she had the half image, as once or twice in her life before, that she rode the back of a black horse, but that had been in dreams and now real flesh and muscle galloped between her thighs.

As she came, her womb gulping in pushes and rushes, returning and returning to the bursting pivot of bliss, the train slowed down. It halted when she did, as if the whole world had stopped. For a second she did not know his name, perhaps not her own. Where were they? Would he kill her now? But he groaned and spasms shook him, and they were only in Europe, somewhere, and he was only a man, after all.

Chapter One: Having Arrived

By the time they reached Paris, Raoul had bought her betrothal ring.

It was a diamond. A polished diamond, not cut, for he said he thought that large cut diamonds were vulgar. This stone was soft as a rainy moon. It was set in twisted old dark gold.

In the shadowy basement room with barred windows, where first she tried it on, Anna was impressed. It was what she would have called *antique* jewellery. She could imagine thieves cutting off her finger to get it. It did not seem it could ever belong to her, but nothing ever had. Either seemed to, or had, belonged. He would take it away, or ask her only to wear it sometimes, locking it in a safe. This did not happen.

In a way, the house was like the ring. Like the ring, as it *seemed* to be: hers... not hers... Nothing to do with her. Big. Polished, though.

Or no, the house was simply somewhere they went to.

She had never been in England. She had only read about it, and looked at pictures.

This was like a Landscape with Country House.

Outside, there had been farms and fields, and then a gateway in a wall, and a muddy drive. The rain was streaming, and against the opaque purple slate of the sky, the horse-chestnuts that lined the drive were a rich, acid and improbable green. There were so many trees. Old cedars and beeches, and oaks, one of which had stood,

Raoul muttered, in the time of a queen called Elizabeth I. Then there was a treeless gap, and the lawns went up baldly to a long terrace, and a house of yellowish stone, with pointed roofs crayoned in on the shadowy light.

And far, far behind, there were hills like small vague mountains.

Anna knew she should be impressed, overawed, or - what Raoul seemed to want - *thrilled*. So she gripped her hands together and said breathless things - How old was the house? What style was it? Wasn't it just like a painting? - to please him.

She was indifferent to it, however. It did not seem real. It was preposterous. She felt like a visitor to some peculiar and perhaps over-rated monument. She would always, she decided, be a visitor, here.

The afternoon arrival was a flurry. Anna had read in novels about such flurries of arrival.

There were a lot of servants. They wore the shiny black of beetles and searing white starched aprons and caps that had a Puritan look. A tall fat man, with a horseshoe of grey hair round his bare scalp, was the butler. They all, saving the butler, had some sort of accent. Anna had spoken English and French most of her life, and other languages, where needed, fluently. But the accent of the servants she found difficult and excluding. She stared at them, feeling her eyes popping with strain, and only realised after, they had simply been welcoming her.

All the maids curtseyed - a bob, it had been called. And the butler nodded.

Anna might have wanted to laugh, but instead it depressed her. She was so tired. The journey had been in quite easy stages, until the last two or three days. Then train succeeded train, and boat, train, and train, boat, with dull miserable little stops between, hotels creaking in the wind, fires quick-lit that smoked and warmed nothing. Sandwiches, cold meats, things you didn't want, being worn out, and only a few snatched hours of sleep before starting off again. Raoul so relaxed. She trying to be bright.

How swiftly, Anna saw, she had got used to food and proper beds, to rooms even, shelter. How blasé and thankless she was, turning from the sour cheese, the smoky fire. She was not, though, used to Raoul. Sometimes he woke her during the journey, making love to her. Once he had come into a bathroom and simply begun stroking her, *there*, at her core. Until she climaxed with a sudden shudder.

After the last soul-rattling train, which was freezing cold, came the car ride, to the house, which took two hours.

When the episode of servants was over, Anna went up to bed. Raoul had explained she would not need to meet anyone until dinner.

The bedroom was like a cavern. What else? She did not look at it. The fire was hot; they had run her a bath. Three maids, standing in a row. She sent them out. She was too polite, of course. They had faces like eggs, blank.

She stepped into the bath, crawled out, crawled into the enormous bed under its yellow tester. Was gone.

Someone was saying something incomprehensible to her. "No," said Anna. "I can't. No."

The voice spoke again. It was soft and female. Anna looked under her lids.

A sly, slim fox's face, with a bonnet of horrible starched linen. A maid. "What is it?"

The maid said something Anna couldn't properly understand. But it was about getting up, and someone coming - the housekeeper? - or a dress...

"Oh, thank you. Yes. Thank you."

Anna realised she had slept as usual naked, and the maid was here, waiting for her to get up, or so it seemed. Yes, the maid was waiting. Her slim hands were folded on her apron. Pale reddish hair slid back under the nasty bonnet. Her eyes were tawny under half-lowered lids.

"Thank you. I'm sorry. I'd like you to wait outside."

The fox maid bobbed. She said, "Missus sayum to lug artor you. Till as missus picks aton other." This was what it sounded like, anyway.

"Oh, I see. But I'd like you to go out for a moment."

The maid looked up, at her. Eyes not tawny, yellow as the tester and counterpane. What awful eyes. Like a cat's - or a *goat's*.

"What's your name?" said Anna, almost in a panic.

"Sister," said the maid. Perhaps.

"Very well - Sister," Anna was firm. "Please go out and shut the door."

"Ysm."

Anna felt close to trembling. This was all so silly. She did not know what to do here, had never lived in a house with any servants beyond a slovenly cook here and there, or some skivvy who did everything. But the fox maid called sister was going at last. The door shut.

At a scramble Anna left the bed. She ran across the room to the bathroom where she recalled her robe had been left lying.

The bath stood on iron legs, *paws*. The water was still

in it and the room felt steamy though chill. When she let the water out, the bath made evil noises.

There was this housekeeper coming. And then dressing for dinner, one of the glaucous dresses Raoul had bought her.

Anna tied the robe. She wiped the mirror. She cleaned her teeth at the inset basin, white and shell-shaped. The taps were brass, polished like gold, and in the form of gryphons' heads. Like those things on the roof - gargoyles.

She was smoking a cigarette and brushing her hair with the tortoiseshell brush, when the housekeeper brought the fox maid back into the room.

The housekeeper had no accent at all.

"I regret," said the housekeeper, "Mr Raoul's telegram arrived very late. Things aren't as ready as I'd have wished." She wore a burgundy red dress and a little watch pinned on her right breast. Her hair was like lacquered ebony, probably dyed. She had the face of a chorus girl playing a housekeeper. She smiled. Her false teeth were very good, but somewhat discoloured. "Sister will do her best for you."

"Sister? Is that really her name?" Anna blurted. "Sister" merely stood there, goat eyes down.

"Lily Sister," elaborated the housekeeper.

Anna felt dispirited. "What happens next?"

The housekeeper laughed in a tight small way. "Sister will help you dress. Dinner is normally at eight-thirty."

"I prefer to dress myself," said Anna. "I don't need anything, thank you."

When they were gone, Anna dressed. She powdered her face and touched her lips with red. Raoul did not like her to use mascara; he had compared her long pale lashes with moths' wings.

She anticipated all the time that he would come in. But he didn't.

From the windows of this room in the back of the house, the lawns swept to a beech coppice, and then away up to the sides of the mountain-hills, now patched with mist or fog. Rain dripped, and the light was going.

There were some cows in a pasture over a sort of narrow river. They moved about sullenly. They seemed undecided.

What was she doing here?

Raoul had once or twice referred to his family, and then just as ordinary people did: "*My Family.*" But they had a title. Then again, it wasn't used. The family name was Basulte.

Raoul had told her so little. But he had promised to tell her nothing, and to ask nothing. And he never had asked Anna anything fundamental or finite. His questions had been limited to such things as "Where shall we go for breakfast? Do you like this wine? Will you put on that necklace for me? Are you comfortable? Do you enjoy it when I kiss you here?"

She knew nothing about him, or about the house and the Family. Only names like England, and Basulte.

Anna was terribly nervous, and yet, adrift in the unreality, she didn't care. Did not care what she felt or what anyone felt. Did not mean to impress. Her impulse was only not to cause a dramatic scene. That had always been one of her goals, for a long time. Scenes were dangerous.

She came down three long corridors, and through the

gallery with suits of armour and oil paintings of costumed persons, men with swords, women with little dogs. The electricity had been switched on, and the hanging lamps were alight, making the gallery stark and its strip of red carpet jump at her eyes. Beyond the gallery was a sort of annexe with doors opening off, and then the top of a curving stair, marble and wood and gilding, just like a European hotel.

The stair ended below in a glass room. It was called an orangery - oranges had been grown in it once, in the 17th century, apparently. It looked now fabulously cold, and the harsh light made tall plants and wicker tables resemble cut-outs of thin card.

Beyond was the room Raoul had mentioned to her earlier. The salon. He had drawn her a map of the route. It was perhaps a test of her skill, to see if she could find her way.

The salon was all dull dark green, with flares of blood-scarlet - roses, and some other flower, that looked African, glassware, wines in decanters.

A fire was burning in the ample fireplace, on this filthy English summer evening.

And about the fire they sat. The Family. Had they been waiting for her? Or were they utterly indifferent? Had they been told she had dismissed the maid: how eccentric and lower-class - the English were reportedly obsessed by class, like Hindus.

They were like a pride of animals up on their home rock.

No. Not animals. They were not, at all, like that.

Nor like a family. Yet they were - a group, a *band* - and they were very alike, you saw this at once. They were all - like Raoul.

That was natural, wasn't it? A familial similarity. His father, his mother, a sister, a brother. But then, there was one who was the sister's husband, surely, or had Anna misremembered? And he too was indistinguishable.

The table-lamps glowed on their black, smooth hair, in their black clear eyes. They were all impeccably dressed, black and white for the men, shades of jade and rose for the women. A few precious stones, gold.

Only Raoul was not there.

Raoul, who had brought her here, given her a ring and a map, as if in a fairy story.

At her entrance, no one had altered. The three men had already been standing, smoking at the fireplace. The two women remained seated.

Their *heads* had turned. Their faces were arrested. Two of the men had been smiling, and smiled still. The others were expressionless.

Anna poised before them. She felt naked in her expensive underclothes, dress, shoes, her diamond.

"Oh," said the woman in the rose-red, "Raoul is too bad. He was to have brought you down."

Anna realized, she should have waited, to be *brought*.

"I'm sorry, I..." She closed her lips hurriedly.

One of them – Raoul's father? - said, "It's so nice you didn't wait. Anna, if I may call you that."

"Of course," she said. She did not know how to address him, since Raoul had not explained.

Across the room, the butler stood, and a maid, and a young boy in black, a footman, by a sideboard that was laid with bright bottles and decanters. When Anna glanced at them, the butler nodded his head, the footman bowed, the maid bobbed, and the bottles flashed.

The man who had spoken to Anna walked over to

the sideboard and inspected it, as if he had forgotten it was there. When he did this, the maid cowered away into the wall. That was no exaggeration. She cowered. But it wasn't fear. It was some excessive show of respect. The footman stood, head bowed now, as if in church.

Raoul's relation made a pass over the array of drinks.

"We have everything, Anna. What would you like?"

She wanted absinthe, she thought. That wouldn't do. And despite the foolish boast, they wouldn't have it. These English were supposed to drink sherry, were they not? She asked for sherry.

Something in the way she pronounced the word must have made the woman in jade-green laugh sharply. Or it was a coincidence?

Startled, Anna stared a second at her.

Which of the women was Raoul's mother? They looked virtually the same age. And the men were equals, but for the one who had spoken to her, and had a grey line in his hair. This was too fanciful. The light was dazzling and deceptive.

The fatter woman was probably the elder one, the mother, Raoul's mother.

The maid came with a sherry on a tray and bobbed, her head held down. Anna took the drink, which was small, in a thimble, a shard of crystal.

They - the Family - had already had their drinks.

The sherry was dry, almost salty. Two sips and it was gone.

"I wonder," said Anna; they looked at her. "I wonder... where Raoul is?"

"He went out riding," said the woman in green. "In this rain." She sounded for a second nearly normal.

"As a boy, horses were his passion," said the other

woman. "But he can't be long, tonight."

Anna disconcertingly recalled those moments proceeding orgasm on the train, the horse galloping between her thighs. Did Raoul once have such a fantasy?

One of the other men came up to her and offered her a cigarette. She took it and the butler was there at once, lighting it for her, stepping between them like an invisible air. Anna thanked the butler, and the woman in green laughed again. But again, that might be nothing.

On the mantelpiece an ormolu clock, with nymphs and a rayed sun, chimed the half hour. Anna had been shown a clock rather like that, in Prague. Figures had danced slowly round it. But she had been crying, and not seen it clearly.

"Shall we go in?" said the man with the line of grey in his black hair. He nodded to one of the other men - Raoul's brother, his sister's husband. "Since Raoul is so late, take Anna in, won't you?"

"My great pleasure," said this other Raoul, stepping up to her.

My God, on his arm, half impossible to tell the difference.

But the fat woman was the Mother. She was stiff when she got up, and the maid assisted her. And the woman allowed herself to be assisted, as if by a mechanical thing, and the maid fell away from her, when no longer needed, like a discarded shawl.

The dining-room - the *small* dining-room - was red, with flutes of green, plants, candles, glass. There were green vegetables on the plates, and bloody meats.

Raoul did not arrive. No one mentioned his absence again. They spoke of him, however.

"I suppose Raoul took you to Versailles. Oh, what you missed, Anna. A heavenly place."

"When Raoul was travelling with you, you'll have noticed, he gets tetchy if kept waiting. Tetchy - oh, that means bad-tempered. You didn't notice? Ah, well, Anna. Your charms doubtless softened his rage."

They did not refer to her engagement, or impending marriage. They asked her nothing about herself.

Later they opened the curtains. That is, the servants opened them. Outside was the terrace, lit by electric lamps held up by statues, and rain glittering and prancing on the stones. The women did not separate from the men.

Then they migrated jointly back to the salon. One of the men put records on a gramophone. He danced with the woman in jade-green, the cosy, liquidly-shuffling dance from America that was only intimate, asking no footwork. Her husband? There was a little scar through his left eyebrow. Anna could memorize him from that.

They never told her their names. She didn't ask.

Raoul did not come in.

Should she pretend to be worried, make a slight gentle feminine fuss?

At ten they began to go to bed, or off about their own pursuits. They said to her, "Good-night, Anna. Do sleep well."

She sat alone in the salon, got up and walked into the dining-room. Rain glittered and pranced.

The butler, the maids, the footmen, (there had been two at hand for dinner) stood at their stations.

Hotly embarrassed, she suddenly stupidly grasped she was imprisoning them, they were having to wait, to wait on her.

She left the rooms and went through the dismal black-windowed orangery of cut-outs, upstairs, along the gallery, through corridors to her bedroom.

The fox maid was standing by the bed like some awful useable machine, a trouser-press or mangle.

"It's all right, Sister. Thank you."

"Sull I undo yemiss?"

"No. Thank you. Goodnight."

When Sister – *Sister!* - sibling, nurse - had gone, Anna threw off her clothes and left them on the carpet. She knew from novels this room was hers, not *theirs*. Her betrothed had an apartment elsewhere.

Anna woke, swimming. She was lying on her side, and an anemone had fastened on her breast, and was drawing her up by silver strings through the nipple. On the other breast, feathers tickled irresistibly.

Anna unsealed her eyes.

"No... stop... where were you?"

"I've been away from the house so long. I wanted to see it so much. Sorry about that. And I was so tired then, I went to sleep. Rotten of me. Your first night. Forgive me?"

His other hand strummed sweetly the instrument of delight between her legs.

She fell back and he mounted her, firming into her, filling her full. Ripples of swirling ecstasy. Unbearably she came, arching her throat and back, as he rode on the crest of her, slapping her hips and choking her name.

At the house in Preguna, Anna had typed the old professor's manuscript. The manuscript was very long, about one thousand pages, in long hand. It was a study of certain, to Anna, obscure schools of thought, starting in third century Greece, encompassing Renascence Rome and Coptic Egypt, ending up in Paris and Alsace. Apparently. Sometimes the professor would wander in and hand her a new sheaf of papers, which were to be inserted, say, after page five hundred, paragraph six. So the manuscript was not complete, was growing, and might never be finished with.

Some afternoons, when the warm dusty sun shone through the windows, whose shutters had been thrown back, Anna typed in paroxysms of yawning, voluptuous and nearly painful, her eyes streaming with water. And twice, when the professor entered, he saw this, and asked if she were crying.

"No, no. I have a little cold."

The house was tall and crooked, packed between other tall, crooked houses, all the colour of old brown bread. The road outside was cobbled, and at the end of the vista was an ancient horse trough and a clock-tower with a narrow blue dome.

If the professor asked her to stay for supper, they ate in a brown back room, waited on by a big woman with a bun. There were cats who lived in her kitchen, but only for the mice. The professor allowed the cats to come up and sun themselves at the window on a chair's back, but if Anna tried to stroke them they ran away, or scratched her.

Usually, after the supper, they had strudel, which the woman had made. It was wonderful strudel, but Anna always suspected the woman put things into Anna's piece. Once there was a hard grain, which might have been glass, and once a bitter taste, and later Anna's stomach had hurt. But she ate the strudel nevertheless.

When the sun went and the rooms darkened, the professor would give Anna a liqueur.

All evening, he would have talked about poetry or philosophy, ideas and people she had never heard of, but she knew herself to be quite ignorant. Then again, he might be making it all up.

In the darkness, he would sit down in the big armchair, and ask her to sit on his knee. He liked her to sing a little song he had taught her, about woolly lambs, gazing away from him but at the same time fiddling gently with his organ.

After about a minute, though now and then it was longer, he would come, with a slight jolt, like a hiccup. There was very little moisture, and this he quickly wiped away with a handkerchief.

Then they would have coffee, and she would go out on to the street, to catch the tram.

Those warm evenings, the dust settling on a nine o'clock breeze, the smell of flowers from the public gardens thick as honey. She was never nervous, even passing through clouds of drunken sailors from the dock, who whistled and called out to her. She didn't mind them. If they had caught her, she would simply have given in. There was only trouble if you resisted, so she had heard. She even smiled, if they did.

Out of the dimness of evening, the tram would come rattling; chrysanthemum yellow with lights.

Once a young man on the tram had picked her up. They went to a café and drank a schnapps. He had a birthmark over his forehead and one cheek, and sat with his hand covering it, as he had tilted his hat to try to hide it on the tram.

At last he said, "Are you always so easy? Don't I disgust you?"

Anna shook her head. He had an attractive face, and the mark was a clear sumptuous red. It reminded her of warrior's paint before a battle.

"Oh, you liar," he said. He tossed back the schnapps - for a second she had thought he would toss it in her face. "You whores will take on anyone. Dirty bitch."

She saw he hated his body so much that he had come to hate proportionately anyone who would tolerate it. To tolerate him must be the sign of a deviant.

Anna realised she should have left well alone, but this was something that she never seemed to do.

After he left her, Anna walked the rest of the way to her lodging. Above her twisted street, the stars were burning bright and coldly blue.

When she thought of Preguna, she usually remembered first the stars, and the trams, and often the professor, and then the man with the birthmark.

When she woke in the morning, the bed was empty but for herself. But she had woken because two of the maids were rustling in through the door.

In the half-dark of the closed curtains, they looked undeniably malign in their beetle black, and starched headdresses. Two preying insects that perhaps had meant to crawl up on the bed.

But one said, "Goomorna, muz," and they both

executed their absurd little 'bob'.

Before Anna could say a word, the speaking one glided to the curtains and flung them wide.

Excruciating light exploded about the room.

Anna winced.

The other maid seemed to be trying to haul her to a sitting position. It was too late, Anna's white breasts with their pink buds had been popped out over the sheet. The maid did not react at all, only immediately brought the robe from the bed's foot and draped it over Anna.

Now there was a breakfast tray on her knees. Good heavens. The English breakfast. Toast in a silver cage, a silver teapot and china cup, butter and jams, and the huge warm plate, covered by a silver bulb.

They shook and fluttered the napkin, and laid it on her like an honourable flag.

The light from the windows was not so bright, in fact. A day pale grey as a dove, the ghosts of the foggy mountain-hills.

"Issum ovuthan you reguire?" asked one of the maids.

I don't require most of it, Anna thought. She said, "Thank you. Oh, yes. Thank you."

They hovered. What now? Would they try to feed her? She had penetrated their accent rather better today. Or were they enunciating more carefully for her dunce's ear?

"Do go," she said, "please do. Thank you."

When they were bobbingly gone - did they titter in the corridor? No, they were machines - Anna pushed the tray aside. She went into the bathroom to relieve herself, clean her teeth and wash her face.

When she came back she inspected the hidden plate

with startled wonder.

There were two thick slices of crisped ham or gammon, two perfect poached eggs, some sort of garnish, like a sort of solid sauce mixed with cream, black mushrooms.

She ate the toast and drank all the tea, then flushed the eggs and mushrooms and garnish down the lavatory. She folded the gammon into the napkin. There might be a dog she could feed it to. Didn't the English always keep dogs? Dogs, and horses.

Where was Raoul? There was one black hair lying in her bed, like a token. Had he pulled it out for her on purpose?

She thought of Psyche in the legend, who never met her lover by day, only during the exquisite passions of the night, in blackness, unseen.

Psyche's lover had been a god. When she found that out, he left her.

Anna bathed, and dressed in a day dress bought in Paris, far too plain and chic to be suitable here.

With the napkin of pig-meat in her bag, she left her room and went out through the house by the route the map had shown her yesterday.

But she took a wrong turning, somehow. It had seemed straightforward, the previous night. The gallery did not appear, whatever the case. The corridors led into and out of each other, papered in heavy damask, red, cream, gold, fleur de lys and Tudor roses, or so she thought...

There were bewildering windows, now looking out to the drive and parkland, now back at the mountains and the fields where the lorn cows meandered by the river, next into a walled garden with broken roses clambering everywhere, their cups smashed by coarse rain. It was drizzling again.

Once a black and white maid approached, scuttling. Not one Anna had seen before, but there were doubtless dozens here, in this large mansion. Upstairs maids, downstairs maids, 'tweenies for the between-stairs - whatever that meant. Maids for scullery and kitchen, assistants to the cook who had fried up the gammon, whisked the sauce-thing. And ladies' maids, like Lily Sister. Then there were footmen, boys of this and that. Grooms for the horses. A whole regiment. An army.

"Oh - excuse me. I'm lost," she said to the maid, who had already bobbed, and cowered her face away as if to pass in terror, then brought it reluctantly back to attend. "I'm trying to get to the stairs..."

"Tuz thaway, mss," said the maid, pointing the way Anna had been going.

"Thank you so much. Thanks."

Bob. Scuttle. The creature turned the corner, vanished.

But Anna still did not come to the stairs, or only to a smaller stair that led up, and this she unwillingly took.

Then she was in a corridor damasked light green, and then there was an open door. A man came out. Raoul's brother, or the husband of Raoul's sister. No, not that one, for that one, recollect, had the tiny scar through his left eyebrow. Brother then.

He was so *like* Raoul. The black eyes and smooth black hair, the long chin and aquiline nose and lips neither thin nor full, so well-shaped, made for kissing, just as Raoul's were. The figure too. The body. And the hands, with their shortish, capable yet sensitive fingers, and broad palms. And this one, the brother, had a ring on his finger. A dull gold signet. Another identifying mark for future reference.

He smiled gravely at her. Not put out, apparently. "Hallo. You're exploring?"

"I'm lost."

"Of course."

They began to walk together along the corridor. Probably this was not as curious as it seemed.

"I hope you slept well," he said.

"Yes, thank you."

The corridor gave on another short flight of steps, with a runner, and then they were in a greenhouse, a glass conservatory perched up on a tower, perhaps, for it commanded views on every side. Water struck and beaded on the panes and birds flew endlessly over. The wind had risen. It coiled and uncoiled, making a sound that Anna could only describe as a whistle, yet that wasn't really it.

"You can see for miles," he said, "on a clear day."

"Yes. Are those mountains?"

"The locals call them mountains. They're hills."

"And the cows."

"Yes, there are cows."

He offered her a chair, and sat facing her across a table. The conservatory was quite cold, but in sunlight would be scaldingly hot, for the roof was also pure glass. The rain slashed, made the noise of thrown dried peas, or small bullets.

On the table were books, about thirty or forty of them, and cigarettes, and a decanter of something.

"How are you settling in?" he asked.

Anna glanced at him. She said, quietly, experimentally, "Well, I'm not, very much. I haven't seen

Raoul. I don't even know any of your names."

"Not seen Raoul? But didn't he come up to your room, to say good-night?"

The black eyes were intent, devoid of any subterfuge. She read them, and realised.

She said, "What should I call you?"

"Why don't you..." He smiled again. He had the same beautiful teeth. "Why don't you call me Raoul," he suggested, "Anna."

"I must have done," she said. "Did I?"

"I can't remember. Only your lovely transports. He's very lucky. Do you mind?"

"Raoul must do."

"I'm sorry, Anna, but he won't. Don't you think he might have been somewhere else? That is, if he wasn't with you. I don't mean the stable."

"Another woman," said Anna.

Raoul's brother, who last night had got into her bed, made love to her, left her one black hair, now offered her a cigarette.

"I'm afraid so. Is it an awful blow?"

"Yes," she said flatly, indifferently.

"Do you want to know who?"

"Not really."

"You're used to being treated like this."

Anna let him light the cigarette. She had half anticipated the butler, or someone, would materialize from the glass wall to do it.

"I expect you want me to leave," she said.

Surreptitiously she tried to ease the diamond ring off her finger, but it had tightened into her flesh, and wouldn't come.

"It's not like that," said the second Raoul. "This

woman, it's just someone he's always had. He's faithful to her, in a way. He must have thought you'd understand. But you mustn't go."

The wind slapped the greenhouse. Plants in pots shook and the panes reverberated.

"Perhaps I need to speak to Raoul."

"I regret he's off at the moment, Anna. He's been away some months, you see, and Father had things for him to do. He'll be back by lunch, I'd think."

"Your father's so young," she said, irrelevantly?

"Isn't he," said Raoul, who was not Raoul.

"And your mother."

"Mother had a very expensive face-lift in Switzerland. Sometimes you see it on a woman, and it looks bloody, but she was lucky. She paid the earth for it. They say it only lasts two years. Isn't that sad, Anna? But then you'll never have to worry, I mean, about getting old. You've got such good bones. When you're ninety you'll be stunning."

Anna said, "You all look so alike."

"Yes. We're terribly inbred."

"But your sister's husband isn't a Basulte."

"But he is. A cousin. Just distant enough it was allowed. By the church, I mean."

Anna said, too dramatically she felt, "Can I ask you not to deceive me again, I mean not to come into my room. Until I speak to Raoul."

"Oh, yes. That's understandable. When you get his agreement, will you consent?"

"I don't know." She lowered her eyes. Her pulse was beating, and in her groin quivers of feeling disturbed her. She thought he might seize her and possess her, here in this box of glass, shivering with cold, kicking through the panes...

She stood up.

"I think I'll go down."

"Just a minute."

He reached right across the table and she felt her mouth go dry, her limbs melt. But it was her bag he took hold of. Without asking her, he undid the clasp, and drew out the napkin of gammon.

"You don't want, this, do you? It's rather heady."

"No. I was... going to look for a dog."

He laughed. "We don't have any dogs. Not the doggy sort. I sometimes think of the servants that way. Loyal and useful, obedient, waiting on our whim. I suppose *you* wouldn't ever think like that. You're rational and modern. But I was brought up here."

The meat, laid bare now on the table among the books, glistened with its fawn fats. They both stared down at it for some while, before Anna left the conservatory.

"She's so pale, very blonde, and such a white skin. Even the eyes. And her features. One would never automatically take her for a Jew."

Anna paused, listening.

Out in the gallery stood the Mother and Sister of Raoul. They were posed idly beneath a picture five feet in height, of a big satiny woman in a low-breasted gown, holding a white dog on a leash.

"It's ironic, really," said the Sister of Raoul. "We're so much darker. Yet, no one could take us for Hebrews, could they?"

They chuckled.

The white dog had a horn. It was a unicorn.

"Oh, Lilian," said the Mother to the Sister of Raoul, whose name must be Lilian, "no one *ever* would."

Anna thought of her passport. Anna Moll. Europe seethed with hatred of the Jews. Had always done so. Recall the dense red walls of the ghetto in Venice. The secret mediaeval pits where they had been left to starve, near Warsaw, unless, unless that was a lie.

"But there," said Lilian, Raoul's sister.

Anna came out into the gallery, her heels making a crisp noise. They would have heard her, anyway, and heard her stop.

The other women looked up, unflurried. "Ah, Anna. We take luncheon at one. Shall we go down?"

There were four men at lunch. One of them must be

Raoul. Not the one with grey in his hair, or the scarred one, or the one with the gold signet ring. Anyway, obviously, she could recognise him at once, in the daylight of the small dining-room. Against the plummy reds splashed with green, the *original* Raoul. His nose was a little more crooked, wasn't it, and his hands rather more fine, the fingers longer; one with a tiny dark freckle always under the nail... She was taking note of landmarks, surely.

When she came in between the Basulte Mother and the woman called Lilian, the original Raoul turned to her smiling, and she thought, *Was it all a joke?* But if it was a joke, *what* joke precisely? Had the brother lied? Or had the brother and Raoul devised the lie between them, like a test of female virtue in a play by Shakespeare? Would she fail if she spoke of it to him, or fail if she did not?

She should not stay here. She should find a means to go. But how, where? This had always been the problem.

"You look edible, Anna," murmured Raoul, with the freckle under his nail.

He had, after his first avowal concerning love - or something - at first sight, not mentioned loving her again.

They ate lunch.

The women both wore green. Anna too had selected a green dress. To match the rooms.

During the meal, the men spoke about an estate, presumably the lands of the house. Horses and fields, something about 'gamebirds' in the 'old days'. The husband of the sister called Lilian said something about some drunken affray at the public house in the village.

The sister remarked to Raoul, "You ought to show Anna the village. It's awfully quaint." She added to Anna, "Some of the houses were built in the 15th century."

Anna looked at her. The eyes of the woman were hard as the polished diamond, though black. A mediaeval village, how suitable for the Jewess, who in those days would have been confined behind a wall, or burned for cooking Christian children.

In the harsh pale light, the Mother's face did seem rather odd, young and too tight on the neck, which was itself hidden in an *eau de nil* scarf. Her hands were old, like claws, painted bright red at the tips. Like the hands of a madam.

The Father was not much more than forty, though, Anna thought. Men wore better anyway. They had a natural inclination to the carven and the rough, it was more fitting, this deep line by the mouth, the coarsening skin.

Will I ever be old? Anna glanced at her idea. Whenever she looked ahead, there was only a dim void. She fell softly into it, down and down. It didn't hurt.

The lunch was over. Now there was coffee in the salon.

"Would you like to go to the village, Anna?"

"Why not?"

When they were upstairs, he followed her to her bedroom and went in with her. He pushed her to the wall, pulled up her skirt and dragged away her flimsy knickers like paper. He was finished in much less than a minute.

This surprised her, not the act, (she had known it happen this way before), but from him.

"I'm so sorry, Anna. That was selfish and brutish. Please forgive me. I just couldn't wait. It's been foul, not having you."

Anna stepped from her ruined underclothes and drew down her skirt. She made a decision. Or, she made a decision as she always did, on the moment's spur, not reasoning.

"But you were here last, night. You came in when I was asleep."

Raoul too was adjusting his garments. He was flushed and lit a cigarette. "Oh. That."

She waited. Then she said, "Do you mean it didn't count?"

"It wasn't enough."

"But - it was *you*?"

He shot her a look, grinning. "Who do you think?"

She went into the bathroom and cleaned herself. When she came out, he was sitting on the window seat gazing out at the overcast, the hill-mountains, cows.

"You know," said Raoul, "my family don't always behave as they should. I should have warned you, Anna. It was remiss of me."

"How don't they?" she said.

"It's in their blood. This lord of the manor thing. They behave like potentates. Basultes have owned this land since the Conquest."

"Which... conquest?"

"Centuries ago. You can see, we're that black Franco-Celtic Norman strain."

"I heard your mother and sister," Anna said, "discussing my blonde Jewishness."

"Take no notice. None of them has ever been out of this house. Well, I mean, they have, physically, to France, Italy, Switzerland, that sort of thing. But they don't *see* anything. What do they know?"

She said, "Do you wish I wasn't here? Shall I go away?" When she had said it, she waited in suspense, nearly terror, not knowing what she dreaded the most, his rejection, or some vow of need.

But Raoul said nothing, and then he said, "If we're going out, let's do it soon, Anna. My father wants to talk over some business with me after four."

They walked. She had been lent galoshes and a hideous waterproof and a sort of sou'wester, the sort of hat fishermen wore, apparently, or was that the men who *rescued* fishermen?

The housekeeper had overseen the maid who brought these items. The maid was Lily Sister.

Anna had been struck suddenly by the names, Lily Sister, *Sister* Lilian.

"What is that girl's name?" she asked Raoul, as they clumped along the muddy, squelching drive.

"Which girl?"

"The maid with the boots and coat."

"Let me think. God knows. Oh yes. Lilith Izzard."

"Izzard." She had thought for a second he said *lizard*.

"Lily," he said. "They call her that, I believe."

Anna breathed the wet tree-dripping country air. It had an English smell, what she would have expected.

"I don't know the names of any of your family."

"Oh, Anna. So much to remember. Poor girl."

"I didn't forget. They didn't tell me."

"Oh, they must have. Never mind."

The long flags of chestnut leaves, grainy and veined as ageing skin, painfully green; the wet flopping down in enormous droplets. Black clouds bubbled over the sky.

"Your sister is called Lilian," said Anna.

"Mm," he said. "Margaret Lilian."

Anna left a gap. She said, "Your brother told me he was called Raoul." Another snap decision.

But Raoul only pulled a stick off a bush, and slashed with it at other bushes, and the high grass now bordering the drive. Live leaves tattered and tore from the stick and were lost.

"William. He's named for my father."

Anna considered the bouquet of names. Something stirred incoherently in the depths of memory. The Conquest of England, the Norman Conquest. Hadn't the man who led that invasion been called William? Perhaps William was not the name of Raoul's brother.

Water splashed up and entered the galoshes, and now she walked in two cold puddles.

There was the odour of soaked earth, dead clandestine things rotting, springing plants.

At the end of the drive, they turned out of the tall gate into a lane. The dreary fields folded away, and trees in patches, and in the distance were smoky woods.

It was a horrible walk, so wet and pointless. And finally, when they had trundled through several lanes, and clambered over stiles of black wet wood, and a bull had leered at them, black himself as Tartarus, they got down into the sodden village.

Sallow houses with ebony timbers and fish-bowl windows ran up the street. Flowers lay flat, smashed by rain, in gardens. There was a church, with flinty, scratchy-looking walls, and with a big square tower that had a clock on it.

"The bells ring all Sunday," said Raoul. "It gets on my nerves, rather."

He took her by the pub, which had a sign of an armoured knight killing a pretty doll-like dragon, strangely similar to a picture she had seen by Ucello. "I'd buy you a drink, but if they see me they get in a lather.

The beer's good. It's a pity."

Anna pictured them, jumping into a vat of lathery beer.

Two wet cats were yowling by the pub's garden wall. Roses grew in tubs, but the heads were off and on the street like pools of cerise paint. A horse stood tied by the horse trough, swishing its tail as if the drizzle starting were only flies.

"You seem different here," she said softly.

"Mm. I'm sorry. It's not much fun for you. There are things I must do, to please my father. Then, maybe we'll go up to London. You'd like that? Restaurants, and the theatre. Cinemas too. And you can buy your trousseau."

"For the wedding."

"Yes, darling Anna. For the wedding in that grim church we just saw."

She wondered if she should confess to him, at this crucial and quite inappropriate moment, that she could never bear him a child. She felt no responsibility really. A plan of escape was almost before her now. For in London, that great city, she could give him the slip.

"I'm a foreigner," she said.

"Your English is virtually perfect," he answered.

The cats began to fight, rolling over and over, screaming, and a woman ran out of the inn or pub to throw a pail of excess water over them.

"Good day, Mrs Lizard," said Raoul.

No, he had said *Mrs Izzard*.

The sign of the lizard-dragon swung in a glancing wind, and the woman gave a little bob to Raoul, her sly lemon eyes slipping over Anna.

"G'dee, Masur Basul. Issis or young lady, mi do I be boldun ask?"

"Yes, Mrs Izzard. My lady, Anna."

The cats, sopping wet, snaked between Anna's legs, and she felt them even through the galoshes. Counterpoint, warmly, Raoul's semen ran down her thighs in an abrupt laving.

Mrs Izzard, the mother perhaps of Lilith, displayed her few teeth. A smile out of prehistory, placatory and trustless.

"Willastup in, Masr? Take a pint?"

"No thanks, Mrs Izzard. Not now."

"The yun lady loogs tired, she duz."

In the inn or pub was darkness. Nothing moved. A den, waiting, for the she-fox to bring in her prey.

"Good day," Raoul said again, guiding Anna up the lugubrious street.

Anna *was* tired. Enervated. They had the return walk, too. The air was not refreshing.

At the top of the village were copses of trees, and fields, and Raoul plunged off into the grasses, swinging his vicious slaughtered stick.

As they strode on, Raoul took off his hat, and shook it. She glimpsed the back of his neck.

Had that little mole always been there, surely she would remember it?

"We can go round this way," he said. "It's uphill. A bracing walk. We'll be back like the children in the story, in time for tea."

Later on, after the scones and muffins and teacakes and iced cakes and fruit cakes, he took her mildly aside.

"Mrs Pin says you won't let the girl dress you."

"*Who* says?"

"Mrs - the housekeeper. If you don't like that one

maid, you can have another. Just say. That's what they're there for, to look after you."

"Your servants."

"*Our* servants."

"William said," said Anna, "he thought of the servants as dogs. Obedient and loyal."

"Oh, William. Just do as I ask, Anna."

"But what do you ask?"

"Silly girl. Let the maid see to your clothes and hair and so on. You see, Anna, you've insulted her in a way. It's her function to wait on you. If you say no, you're - frankly, you're slapping her in the face."

One evening at Preguna, when she hadn't gone to the Professor's house, Anna was sitting in a café, drinking coffee, and the young man with the birthmark came in.

Anna looked away at once. Then, in a while, she heard him walk over. His shadow fell between her and the sun.

"May I - may I sit down?"

"Oh, yes," she said, not looking.

The chair scraped, and he was facing her, over the table.

"I wish to apologise to you," said the young man. "You were very nice to me, and I was very rude."

"Yes," said Anna. She did not look.

"You see," he said, "it's hard for me. No one," he said, "can look me in the face. But then you did. And I'd had a drink or two. What can I say?"

"It's all right," Anna said.

"Excuse me, then," he said.

47

He was getting up again, and she raised her eyes. There he was, his hat inadequately tilted to conceal the silky-mulberry stain. His hair was very fair, almost white on that side. His face was narrow, fine as a poet's. He had dark blue eyes, the right one, cradled in the mark, tinged faintly with rose, like an alabaster lamp.

"You see," he said, halting midway, "you're doing it now. You're looking at me."

"I'm sorry," said Anna.

But he was sitting down again. He said tensely across the table, "What do you see?"

Anna reached out and put her finger lightly on his lips.

"You. What else?" Then his face sank, dropped. His eyes were old. She said quickly, "I didn't mean to upset you."

"I must get up and go away," he said.

Just then the girl arrived, and Anna said, "We'll have two brandies, thank you."

The girl went. A tear ran out of the alabaster eye. The young man caught it deftly on his hand. "Sometimes that happens. It's a weakness. This - thing - on my cheek. It looks as if a woman had slapped me in the face."

Anna laughed. She shook her head. "How vain you are."

He stared at her. Then the brandies came, and they drank them. Ten minutes later they parted, but he stumbled near the doorway, and Anna had the urge to run and help him. However, she stayed where she was.

Chapter Three: Waiting, and Its Consequences

Several days passed in the English House. They were the same in almost every respect, peaceful and boring and uncomfortable, fraught with something like a high-pitched singing note, scarcely to be heard, never quite dying away.

It was continually raining. If the rain stopped, that was only for an hour or so. Anna had heard, or read, of these pluvious English summers. It was as if it had to be since someone had decided. The law.

In the morning, about nine, the maids brought the breakfast tray. She had asked to be given only bread, and added she would prefer coffee. But the breakfast did not change very much. There was no more meat, but instead little boiled eggs under silver, bullet-like caps, or a coppery fish - was it a kipper? And there was never coffee, always tea. She became used to it.

She no longer dropped the food down the lavatory but left it untouched on the tray. Perhaps the servants ate these remains, relied on leftovers.

There were russet kitchens in her past, netted in their strings of onions, tomatoes, garlic, and the cook, the single maid, eating huge feasts at the scrubbed table, their shoes kicked off, belching and cackling.

Then Lilith Izzard-Lizard came and ran the bath, and threw in, unasked, handfuls of bath salts, so it smelled like the squashed rose garden after the downpours.

Impervious, Lilith helped Anna out of her robe, like an invalid. Nudity meant nothing apparently. Where had that myth come from, that the English were prudish? But then, the servants were only dogs, beetles, did not matter.

Lilith dressed Anna. She brushed Anna's short pale electric hair. She would repeat this procedure at night, in reverse.

Lilith said nothing unless spoken to.

Anna saw her narrow fox face over her, Anna's, left shoulder, the folded lids, and yellow eyes, the hint of the sandy hair sneaking in under the bonnet of the slave.

"Thank you so much. Thank you. Oh, how kind."

Ghastly. Unbearable, really.

Not that the girl was unwholesome, unpleasant to come into physical contact with. Just this subservience, so sly and slippery. A slavishness relished?

It's just me. I was never waited on. I can't judge.

Lily brushed Anna's suede gloves. Lily had put lavender sachets into the underclothes. Nothing could be kept from your maid. If ever one had to have a hidden thing, one would need a special hiding place. No wonder all the antique bureaux you read of had concealed drawers. No wonder there were secret passages.

One morning the housekeeper - Mrs Pin - entered and asked, directly over Lily's bowed, blouse-sorting head, if Lily were *Adequate*.

"Perfectly," said Anna.

"If there is anything you're not happy with, Miss Moll."

"She's wonderful," said Anna extravagantly. Wretched fulsomeness.

Actually Anna had begun to loathe Lilith Izzard. Doubtless it was mutual.

But: the servants seemed to have no resentments. They came and went like shadows, and if you passed one, it bobbed or nodded or bowed, depending on its lowly position. And if there were several of them, this action was like rabbits bouncing or corn turning before the wind, this idiotic gesture, of self-abasement.

Anna wanted to cry, "Stand up, for God's sake!"

She could imagine their contemptuous surprise. Or would they even have been contemptuous, or surprised?

They waited on the drinks cabinets, the luncheon table, the dinner table. (Not tea, generally; then the Basultes saw to themselves.) The servants carried things about, circumspectly.

They were like automata, which ran all day, and almost all night too, for she had asked Raoul uneasily about their schedules, and learned of the seventeen or eighteen hour stints, beginning before the light and extending beyond the light. Generally unseen, this scurrying and scraping and pattering and creeping. Those tireless exhausted arms and knees, thrust against and into tubs of washing and potato peelings, bowed to rub the floors and bent to clean the grates. (She was only able to question Raoul now and then, following lunch. Despite the previous day, the men were not often present during tea.)

As Anna lay in bed, waking about one or two a.m., she imagined servants crawling through the arteries of the quiet house. They were everywhere. In the midst of anything, sleep, bathing, masturbation, they would knock and step straight in on you.

The house with infested with them, the servants.

On Sunday, dinner was taken at two o'clock, a Basulte tradition, in the Great Dining-Room.

This room was enormous, flanked on one side by windows pierced to the floor as in the smaller dining-room. It was papered and draped in a rich toffee blue. The ceiling had been painted by a minor luminary of the eighteenth century. It was a lighter blue, with clouds: the sky. (Outside the English heaven scowled and urinated on the park.)

To match the Great Dining-Room, a huge side of beef, black without and reddish within, was carved before them. They drank claret. This quickly gave her a headache, but the Basultes swallowed it undaunted.

She had come to see the Father was very greedy. He ate in an ugly mannered way, still managing to stuff his mouth with large forkfuls of food. She had been told by now, (Raoul) the Basulte grandfather, who had begun the peasant tradition of the two o'clock dinner, would stalk straight in from the hunt, reeking of horse, hound and blood, put his feet on the table, tearing chunks by hand off the roast, so aroused was his appetite.

The woman, the Mother, was greedy too, but she ate very slowly, outlasting everyone, going on and on.

Margaret Lilian would get up and go over to the windows to smoke.

Normally, when the midday meal was over, they dispersed, and Anna would ascend to her room to play patience, or to doze. Later she would read parts of a novel taken from the Basulte library. These books were old-fashioned, their language outdated to the point of seeming another tongue, and bound in leather. She would make herself stick at a book until four-thirty, the usual hour for the (unwanted) tea.

After the Sunday meal, at last the Mother-woman rose, casting down her napkin soiled with lipstick. She led the way into another orangery. As they sat among the sullen palms for their coffee, she said to Anna, "Sunday is the day I visit the kitchen. You must go with me, Anna."

Evidently this was a command.

When the coffee was drunk, the woman went upstairs to prepare herself, and returned once more crimson of mouth, her nose floured with powder.

Beyond what was called the Smoking Room, was a door with felt on it, behind a curtain.

The butler held this door open, and the woman walked through and down a stair, Anna following dubiously.

Anna did not want to know any more about the servants.

But this was the understairs, the below-stairs. A curious fact, the servants slept in the attics overhead, and toiled all day down here, under their feet.

The kitchen was such a big room, conceivably much bigger than the Great Dining-Room.

Anna had recalled those rubicund kitchens of the past, the baskets of washing pushed aside, the plants crouched on windowsills. This was not like that.

It seemed they would have had to tidy it, after all the Sunday food, for this - weekly? - inspection.

The long tables were bare as bones and nearly as white. The linoleum floor was still damp in patches. A mousetrap stood sentinel in one corner. Even that looked tidy, the bait of cheese fresh and cheery.

The ovens, which still exuded heat, were clean. A black iron box of fire - a range - had been scoured by devils.

Even the windows shone.

There were no vegetables hanging, only on a table a basket of early apples, a jug of intact roses. Picturesque.

The cook was there, a big fat woman. She wore a

starched dark dress and apron of blue-white. She and the butler were the only ones to keep their heads unbowed. All the rest, clean as new pins, waited in a line, starched and ironed, hands raw from work, heads bent as if for a dire punishment - as if they had gravely sinned. Bobbing, bobbing.

"Very good, Mrs Ox," said the Basulte Mother of Raoul, (Ox? Had she truly called the cook that? But an ox was a male cow of some kind, wasn't it?)

"Thankum, Madum."

"And your dinner was quite good. The meat... a little well-done, perhaps."

"I regretuz, Madum."

"No. Don't trouble. The butcher is probably the one at fault. Just be a little more careful."

The Basulte woman moved along the line of maids and boys, examining their shirts, aprons, their starchiness, seeing presumably that their hands were properly flayed and red enough. One hand she pointed to. "Mrs Ox, are these nails quite pristine?"

Mrs Ox said, fawningly, "Is ona the mushrooms, madum. No hurm."

"Harm isn't the point, Ox."

"No um, Madum. I beg pardon. I'll seeuz she go wont her tea, Madum."

The girl, whose nails looked only torn down to Anna, made no remonstrance. And when the woman added, "Very good," this girl bobbed again, as if she had received her due, some sort of medal.

As they left, the whole roomful was bobbing, like corks. It made Anna seasick.

The Mother smiled at her as they came up from the nether regions.

"You see, Anna."

"About her nails?" asked Anna. "It seemed a pity."

"Yes. They are so dirty if you don't watch them."

No one had spoken, Raoul had not spoken again, about a wedding. Yet, was this instruction so Anna should learn how the great house must be ordered.

I, Anna thought, *the Jew.*

After the Sunday dinner there was to be a supper, but that was at ten.

Lilith told her, coming in the room as Anna slept, and beginning to lay out, unasked, a suitable dress. "M'slilum says wulla golong anin."

Anna shook her head. "I'm sorry - go along... where?"

"Toer room." Lilith Izzard said something else, which Anna didn't catch at all. She didn't know where Lilian's room might be.

Lilith put a paper in her hand. It was a map of the way, drawn in an impatient yet curlicued manner.

Raoul had never, though he had drawn her a map of the route to the dining-room, given her a map of the way to his own room. And he hadn't come to hers since that first - or second - occasion.

None of the men came to the afternoon tea now, in the orangery. But when Anna had not gone either, a maid had arrived to remind her. (Today dinner had eclipsed the tea.)

Anna had lit the fire laid in the grate because the bedroom was depressingly dank. And Anna could visualise Mrs Pin telling her she should not have lit the fire, but rung for someone to see to it. A long velvet tail hung by the mantelpiece, to summon the servants. Anna had never used it. Pulling tails seemed unwise.

Lilith said nothing about the fire. Her hands and eyes, and the beads on the supper dress, glimmered peculiarly in the firelight.

"What's the nearest town, Lily?" said Anna.

The fox maid said a name, but it was incomprehensible and unknown.

"How far are we from London?"

Lilith stared right at her. Her eyes seemed to leave the glim of her face and float luminously, like topazes in the air.

"Lonun? Oh thabee fur off."

It was all very stupid, this, wasn't it? Anna was a displaced person, but she did not need to be a prisoner.

One got into these habits, like carrying heavy laundry, the pressures of what was expected of you, forcing you round and round in a dull trance. Just so she had gone to school day after day, as a child, the school where she could barely speak the language, and the other children ripped her hair. Until the day it occurred to her she need not go, they would not bother, and so all summer, until the next flight, she sat on the hawk-swooped hills, where the olive trees anciently grew, twisted in adolescent gossamer, about the ancient fort. It was simple.

Lilian sat in her apartment. A dressing room opened from it, and two closed doors. It was all done in tones of cream and milk, but the bed was a strawberry.

She sat like a woman in a painting, her Chinese robe of embroidered ochre silk fallen wide open. She was naked.

Her body was plump but not very firm, the breasts

drooping. At her belly's pit the fleece of her hair was a ripe black, shining as if oiled and brushed, permed and even set, like her upper hair.

"Oh, Anna. Do sit. I wanted to talk to you."

It was reminiscent of a harem. The black beetle-dogs of the maids, three, four of them, eddied about her. One did not fan Lilian with an ostrich plume, but instead stoked the fire.

Firelight played over skin and black dresses.

A girl sorting garments, another sewing something in a corner. One mixing cocktails at a lacquer table. There were even olives.

The air smelled of women, flesh and hair, alcohol, scent.

Anna sat down.

Her own dress was black, but the beads were malachite. She turned a little sideways, from the pouting collapsing staring breasts.

"Oh God. You're not embarrassed, are you?"

Lilian laughed, and her vagina *opened*. Just a momentary glimpse. Like a rosy wink.

Anna shook her head.

"Oh good. I know you foreigners can be a bit stuffy. *Oh for Christ's sake...*" Her voice lifted to a shout. "Haven't you found it yet?"

"Noum."

"Hurry up, you arse." It was the maid sorting through the dresses. "Fucking useless," said Lilian. This was another personality, or the inner life revealed. Abruptly she picked up her cigarette case, heavy gold, and threw it directly at the head of the maid bending to the drinks. "Hurry up, fuck you."

The girl was struck. She reeled. But the cocktail did

not spill, and after a second, she was in place again, setting an olive in each glass.

Anna swallowed. She felt dizzy from the blow.

They drank the cocktails.

(Margaret) Lilian began to talk.

She spoke about clothes, how it was impossible to get anything *decent*. She must go to London. Anna ought to come with her. Anna thought of Raoul's pledge, which might be unmeant, as this almost definitely was, wasn't it?

Lilian spoke as if Anna were quite a close friend. Almost as if Anna were of Lilian's class, or status. Whatever her status was. Then again, she assumed Anna would be happy to accompany her, happy to listen. This demonstrated that Anna was an inferior in many ways, socially and humanly, eager for titbits from this more important table.

"Tommy's hopeless." said Lilian. Anna did not ask who Tommy was, for surely he must be the husband with the scarred eyebrow. Lilian went on, "All he cares about is the business." What business? Anna did not ask. "And the Basulte land. He likes the land. That's what he married, after all."

"Do you know," said Lilian loudly, raising her arms for the silk slip to be slipped on, since by now the maids were dressing her. "Our first night, I mean our wedding night, he was downstairs drinking until nearly six a.m. *Six*, I ask you." But she was not asking, only telling. "Hopeless that way, too, of course. But most of them are. Don't you find that? I need three or four gins even to feel like it nowadays. I keep saying, Slow down, Tommy, for Christ's sake. It's not the fucking Derby."

She must be talking about the sexual act. Internally

Anna twitched, not a flicker of pleasure or anticipation, uncomfortable actually.

The leering breasts had hooded their eyes in silk and lace, and now Lilian was being hooked into an old-fashioned cherry-coloured dress.

A maid came and held out a lipstick and a mirror coped in silver. Lilian crayoned her mouth on and on, as if she were eating something. Between layerings, she still spoke.

"I suppose you've had quite an exciting life, Anna."

Was this a question? No.

"God, I almost envy you. They value women on the continent, make them into little goddesses. I bet you could teach me a few tricks. But I wouldn't be able to use them. Wouldn't be worth it, with bloody old Tommy."

Was Tommy old? He hadn't seemed to be.

"Raoul though. I suppose Raoul's all right." The lipstick was finished. Lilian stalked to a pier-glass and manoeuvred in front of it, smoothing down material over her hips. "Not so bad, old girl. Not so bad." So that was the connotation of old here. "Oh. Raoul and I," said Lilian. She thrust her empty glass at one of the maids, "Fill me up. Yes, Raoul... I've no doubt he told you. We've done a thing or two. When we wore nippers, you know. Nippers - the nanny used to call us that. The Nippers."

Mystified, Anna visualised talons; clipping, pincing motions.

"He pulled down my knickers and had a damn good look and I undid his buttons. What a silly little pink shrimp. Probably not like that now. Oh, don't get the idea we did anything *much*," said Lilian, boastfully. "A bit of slap and tickle. God I'm starved."

Anna glanced at the maids, as Lilian and she left the

room. Were they faceless as eggs? Yes, how odd, truly they seemed to be. The way Orientals were said to be, all the same, except that, with Orientals, one instantly saw this statement was ridiculous.

The girl who had been struck by the cigarette case had the angry star of a bruise rising on her forehead. Anna had seen terrible things, disgusting things, but that action, so needless, heedless, had planted in her a seed of nausea. She could not forget, it. It would be wrong to forget it.

Even so, despite the bruise, bobbing, heads bent down.

There were vast cheeses, but without crusts, these had rinds. Their texture was like softish wax. And a cold ham, a salad, loaves, little pies, relishes. Beer.

The English ate such a lot, and so often.

Raoul was there. Ho spoke to her jollily. He was really and certainly changing, even physically, as if to be camouflaged among his kin. He had been pale and slender, serious and quizzical, all across Europe. His face had a sort of flush to it now and looked fuller, and smug. He laughed loudly, and punched the brother, William?, in the chest. "Dashed bugger."

After supper the women played cards in the salon, some complex game, which they said they wanted Anna to join, and said they would teach her, and this she doubted. She replied she had a slight headache.

The men retreated away over the house, to put as much distance as was feasible between themselves and the women. In the Smoking Room they would drink port and brandy, apparently.

The servants moved on oiled runners.

Anna sat in a big chair. She read one of the old novels, which as usual she could barely grasp.

She heard Lilian say, "Anna and I had quite a chat. Oh, quite a conversation."

Then Anna dreamed she had walked all the way to *Lonun*, as savage lower-class characters sometimes did in the novels. It was a conglomerate of spidery towers craning on a purple sky. The Houses of Parliament - she had once seen their picture - floated in a river of zinc.

When she woke, the women played on, drinking whisky and swearing, but not as Lilian had sworn upstairs.

Anna stole cautiously from the room.

Opening her bedroom door, she found a piece of writing paper had been pushed under. On it, another map.

Raoul had not approached her for anything, scarcely to talk. Walks and congress no longer seemed to matter to him, and the phantom of the capital was forgotten.

Nor was the map Raoul's. Nor Lilian's. A new hand, which made sharp black unlinked edges, the writing a scrawl.

But she made out the direction. The way up to the greenhouse glass box on the tower, the place where she had sat with the man perhaps called William, and he had lied or informed her he had been her lover.

His map, then? His invitation?

Anna sat down at the dressing-table. Beyond undrawn curtains - strange, normally they were drawn by now - the cut lawns ran to the sculpted beeches, and then the river sliced the fields and the mountains, which were hills, cuddled the sky, but moonless night had extinguished everything. Out there - might be only an abyss.

Somewhere an English fox screamed. Anna started. It had happened before, and been identified to her. But the sound was frightful, agony or malediction. No wonder such creatures were hunted. They must be insane and very dangerous - worse than wolves. (She had heard strange noises in the park quite often.)

If she obliged William now, he might facilitate her going away, and even help her monetarily. She didn't for a moment credit this. Nor did she think, if she ignored the challenge, she would be left in peace.

She took off the beaded dress, and fumbled, for she had absurdly already got used to the assistance of the maid.

Anna put on a wrap. If anyone found her in the corridors she would pretend she was sleep-walking. She had done this once, elsewhere, and got away with it.

She was a sort of sleep-walker anyway. There was always this compulsion to go forward, through cities, along roads, across the borders of countries. And into events, blindfolded, searching with her hands. How could you not turn the page? Even in the dark.

The corridors however were lit by the powerful electric lights. Anna had no difficulty, and soon enough there was the stair going up.

It occurred to her quite suddenly at this instant, she had not seen the main entrance hall since her arrival. It had a black and white chequered floor as if for a game of chess, and two fireplaces. The walls were hung by swords and other bellicose paraphernalia, and the heads of stags, floretted with antlers. For the country walk though, Raoul had taken her through back rooms with chests and guns.

She could not recall the way at all to the front of the house.

Then she went up the stair and was in the green corridor.

No doors stood open.

When she came to the second small stair, an appalling odour drifted in gusts to her on the condensed air of the house, at first seeming imagined, then returning more solidly. It was sweetish, yet sour, wet - yet dry, *dirty*, unspeakable. She thought of a time in Paris, a dead rat under the floor...

From above, in the conservatory box, began a harsh restless crying and moaning. Someone in awful and relentless pain. Almost more distressing than the fox.

Anna moved up the stair, and the conservatory was before her. It was soft-lit, only an oil lamp burning against the glass, old light, from an earlier era. At first she did not reason out what she saw by its glow.

On the table the books were spilled. The decanter stood unstoppered in a puddle of liquid.

A girl in a black dress lay over the table, her head hanging off the table's end, so Anna saw her upside down. The hair was undone, a tangle of honey straw. Her black dress, the buttons gaping, one round breast brought out, and the rest of her crushed.

She was howling in her delirium. Now and then she gave a mindless cry, not quite like a beast, the beast in the park.

The man lay over and worked on her, inside her. It was one of the Basulte men. In the lamplight, Anna could not be sure which of them.

At every thrust of his body, the girl, sobbing, whining, her eyes shut, her head tossing. Joy or pain? It was impossible to tell which.

She was one of the servants, the slaves. Her apron too flopped to one side, a gasping starched tongue, and the starched bonnet was caught, like a white insect, in the riot of her hair.

On the floor under the table, where they must have knocked them, kicked them, the two slices of gammon Anna had not eaten, nearly a week before, cotton now, putrid, crawled with little wiggling things.

Above the hubbub, his panting, her cries, the colossal *roar* of stench, the rain prickled delicately on the glass roof, in spangles and sequins, the saliva of moonless, watching, avid night.

Chapter Four: Then

Her life had been a series of bizarre little vignettes. There were so many of them, it seemed almost inappropriate to put them all together, and call this mosaic an Existence.

They were scenes from a play, perhaps. Now a child was dragged along a street, a woman running after the man who dragged the child, waving the man's shirt and shouting. A procession with a band and a white goat led on a leash, and a girl standing at the roadside, smiling at the soldiers, her fur coat open slightly, revealing she was naked under it. And the soldiers too tired to notice. There was a woman with flowers in her black hair, or they might be ribbons, lying as if dead in a large rumpled bed whose pillows were decorated with lace. Women with baskets picking olives, fingers gnarled like the trees. A drunken man singing in an orange café.

Always, to everything, a background of movement. Of coming or going away. Train, boats on choppy water. Even a carriage drawn by horses, and mountains pointed up by snow.

Finally Anna came down like a deer to a river, and met Raoul Basulte. But that recent memory was different. It had been removed this side of a pane of thick glass, transparent but impervious. Behind the pane, the other memories, all the vignettes, the *Past*, crouched, bottled up together. And in the midst of them there grew up one tall, tall tree.

The tree cast its shadow away into the distance, back as far as Anna's birth, or so it seemed to her. And forward, over and through the glass partition, into her present, and then again on, into her future, for ever.

Someone ran up the stairs and knocked on her door. The house where she lodged in Preguna was always full of changing people. She did not recognize the boy, which didn't surprise her.

"There's a fat woman downstairs." Anna shook her head. "From your work-place."

"Oh. "

"She says the old man's taken sick. Wants you to come."

Anna shut the door and dressed. She had been sitting in the chair smoking and drinking coffee, which the German woman brought her on Sundays. Outside the sun was climbing the delft blue sky. It was about ten o'clock.

The fat woman was the woman with the bun, who cooked at the professor's house, and perhaps poisoned Anna's strudel. Her face was sulky but frightened, and pale.

"He was taken ill in the night. He said you must go to him."

Anna could not think why. She was an employee, sometimes a sort of toy. Now and then she had felt sorry for the professor, especially after his sad sudden little hiccup-orgasms. At other times she was rather envious. He had a pension, he had his comforts, and was always writing his book, which he seemed to think was important. He had even, after all, found an easy and successful way to vent the slight sexuality still in him.

Then again, if he was dying, which seemed likely, though the fat woman had not said so, she didn't envy him at all.

The shutters were uniformly closed, and outside on the cobbles Anna saw something she had never seen except very occasionally, in her childhood, straw thrown down there, to muffle any noise of traffic.

When the woman saw the straw on the road, she put her hands over her face and wept. Anna waited. She wondered if she should say something. Finally she said, "I'm sorry. You've been with him a long time."

The woman said, through her tears and hands, "He was the father of my child."

Anna was startled.

"Yes, yes. It was long ago. The baby died."

Anna thought, wondering what else she could say. The woman was the professor's cook. Yet she had borne his child.

The woman wiped her face with a handkerchief. She said, "It wasn't love, you understand. We were younger. One night. It was the summer carnival, when they wear the masks, here, and everyone goes mad. He was kind afterwards. He offered to marry me. But he would have lost everything, and I didn't want to. He would have adopted the boy, but *he's* in the cemetery. Only three months old. Not even a person."

"I'm so sorry."

"No, you are not. People say these things. It's nothing to you. And I suppose when the professor is dead you'll expect some money."

Anna had not thought of this. A flickering passed over her mind and stomach, like faint lightning.

"He has nothing," announced the woman

damningly. "The house will go to the government. I shall work in my sister's husband's restaurant, in Bucharest. A long journey. And I hate trains."

They went into the house, which now felt impermanent as a structure formed from pasteboard.

There was the vaguest medical smell, as if something had been swabbed with ether. The brown air was filled with slender lit columns of dust.

Upstairs, Anna found the door of the bedroom ajar. She had seen into it once or twice, sent to fetch something by the professor. It was a big room, but with a large fireplace, the bed canopied, and there were a massive chest and a wardrobe, bookcases, and so on, so that all the space had been claustrophobically filled. There were paintings on the walls, too, dull and sepia, like the rest, hunts and battles, and one of a depressed girl brooding over a letter, clearly marked, in French, *His last words to her*.

The professor lay propped up on pillows. Beside him a draped table massed with little bottles, spoons, a glass. A fly buzzed against the shutter. Anna wanted to go and let it out, but the man's old grey lids groped up and he saw her.

"You're here," he said.

Anna realised drearily that she must now sit down in the chair by the bed. She did not know why he had wanted her presence, and yet she dreaded a long vigil, perhaps confessions of some sort he could not reveal to anyone else.

Anna sat in the chair. Was he dying? Did he know?

"She brought a priest," he said, showing he did. "But I sent him away. No good to me." Then he struggled forward and to her amorphous horror, caught her hand.

"Anna, Anna - I needed you so badly. Only you." A cold wash passed over her skin. What did he want? Oh God, please let it not be he had fallen in love with her. There had been that other time, when she was only fifteen, and having to lie in those arms to comfort, until death came and she was able to pull free... "Anna, listen."

"Yes... what is it?"

"My book..."

She found she was breathing after all. "Your book."

"Take all the pages, Anna, and throw them over a bridge into the canal. Don't miss any."

"The canal."

"Yes. Oh, someone may find one or two. That doesn't matter. They'll be ruined quickly, the canal's so dirty."

She thought how he had worked endlessly, diligently, all the typing, the re-typing, the swathes of pages added.

"If it's what you want."

"Yes, yes. I shouldn't have presumed. If there had been time - but not like this. No one must see."

It was as if he had written something scurrilous or terrible, which might bring down the state.

"But when you're well again," she said, carefully.

"I'm done for," he said, with all the tragedy of a young hero dying in the arms of his lover or most faithful friend. He added, as if to confirm her notion, "The rest is silence."

And then, extraordinarily, she thought he *had* died on that perfect cue. His head fell back, and his mouth opened as his eyes shut.

She got up and ran to the window, and flung aside the shutter and undid the catch, and the fly flew out like his Roman soul.

But downstairs the fat woman was standing with a doctor, pompous in a black coat, and when Anna said she believed the professor had died, the doctor stared at her with sceptical scorn, since only a doctor was able to recognise a death.

In fact, in this instance, he was correct, but by then Anna had gathered up all the manuscript from the typing room. It was remarkably heavy, and she tied the bulging bundle with string, as if for a publisher.

As she came out of the room, she heard the doctor and the professor talking in low elderly voices along the corridor. This jolted her, but she didn't go to see. She carried the manuscript down and out of the house, and walked directly to the canal.

Although it was indeed filthy, under a blue sky the water was like cracked sapphire, and children were sailing small boats. She had to find another bridge, not to sink them. Here she heaved the manuscript over, and a woman in a garden on the farther bank glared at her suspiciously. *She thinks it's my stillborn baby wrapped in newspaper.*

Anna read of the professor's death in just such a journal two days later. It was a patronising and miniature mention. She did not go back to the house and had no further communication from it. He had not paid her on her last two or three visits; now she had no employment at all.

But she ate very little, smoked cigarettes only as a luxury, and had already put by a small sum for stockings and the rent.

Every so often she had gone back to the café near the public gardens where the young man had come in and walked over to her table, the young man with the warrior's stain of birthmark. She didn't think she did this for any particular reason. It was a café she frequented from time to time, on the days she did not go to the professor's house.

Now she would not be going to the professor's house, presumably, ever again, Anna walked to the café every day, although at different times. She would drink coffee and scan the journals for innocuous work, typing, or the walking of rich people's pet dogs, posing even for artists. She had always done these things.

Ten days after she had read of the professor's death, she was sitting in the café in the late afternoon. She had found no work at all, despite once going to a shop which required a typist. (A shop woman in a beige dress to her ankles had told Anna she was too slow and her spelling was 'old fashioned'.)

With no prospect of an upsurge in her finances, Anna had ordered coffee and also chocolate bread, which she spread with white butter and sprinkled with cinnamon.

As she finished the last piece, the café door let in the young man.

He was as she recalled, slim, and a little more than average height. He had a clear, quite beautiful skin, just tanned from summer, and the mark shone like a cornelian in the shade of his hat tilted to hide it.

Either he did not see Anna, or did not remember her, or wished to forget her. He sat across the room in a corner, the birthmark to the wall.

Anna licked her fingers, and watched him covertly. Then she lit a cigarette. But the flash of the match didn't attract his eye. Of course, people constantly struck matches.

Her coffee was all gone. She ordered a brandy.

Visitors to the café came and went. The young man sat in his corner. He drank two long drinks, and read a book. When the drinks were drunk, he closed the book and put it in his pocket. Then he put down some coins on the table and walked out.

He passed Anna's table. He did not see her. She was sure he didn't. His idea of making himself invisible appeared to be to see no one else. She recollected this from the tram-ride where she had first met him. The tram had lurched and he had bumped against her, uttering a low, stifled apology in his musical voice. This was how they had begun to talk.

Anna swallowed her drink. She got up and went to the door, and looked along the street.

Children were running and laughing in the gardens, and birds sang. Somewhere there was what sounded like a hurdy-gurdy playing. The sunlight had left the lower trees, which were draped in shadow, and hit their tops like golden powder.

She hadn't been quick enough, for he was gone. His footsteps didn't show on the street.

Anna returned inside the café. "That gentleman who just left..."

"Which gentleman?"

Anna said, awkwardly, "He has a mark on his face."

But the girl shook her head. "I didn't see."

Anna stood a moment by his corner table. The coins and the glass were gone, but he had deposited the ashes of a cigarette. Anna put her finger into the ash, then brushed it away in irritation.

That night she dreamed she was talking to the corner table. "Which book was he reading?"

"Oh, a clever book. But I can't tell you. I can't read."

"When will he come back?"

"Oh, any day."

"Where did he go to?"

The table said, "Try clocks."

When she woke up, this odd sequence was paint-fresh in her mind. She considered if it had any meaning.

But she had nothing to do, and when she was washed and dressed and had powdered her face, she went out and walked about, first to the armillary clock on the wall of the museum, and then to the black clock on the cathedral over the square.

She thought of the clock-tower at the end of the professor's street, and wondered if that was what had prompted the dream-table's oracular message. Anna did not want to go this way. She imagined meeting the fat cook in the street, and the woman striking her, saying she would get no money from the dead. Or even that at the last the professor had wanted his manuscript, and died in despair because Anna had thrown it in the canal.

Instead Anna wended back towards the café where she had seen the young man yesterday. En route, she entered a narrow passage, whose upper storeys overhung the path. Here, was a dark jeweller's, with silver watches gleaming in the window like ticking eyes.

He stood in the doorway, his hat tilted, the birthmark turned from the sound of her approaching steps.

"Hallo," said Anna. She added softly, because the dream had been magical and therefore it must be all right, "I knew where to find you."

He half turned back, then darted his head away.

"Who are you?" he said. But she knew now he remembered her.

"Aren't the watches strange," she said, "they all say a different time."

"Yes," he said. The clear side of his face had faintly blushed. Something moved in Anna's heart, and something ached a moment in her spine, first behind her head and then at the base of her pelvis.

"Were you buying a watch?" she asked.

"No... no. I do the old man's books. His takings. His eyes aren't good."

Anna was always impressed by people who could add up, subtract. She collated the other remark more slowly. He did not like to be seen, so poor eyesight might be of great use.

"But you were leaving," said Anna.

"Yes. I'd finished."

"It's so hot," said Anna. "Shall we have a drink?"

"No. I have to catch the tram."

They walked together, not hurrying, along the passage.

Neither spoke, like shy children. But some water had been spilled across the way, and when they came to it, he took her arm gently. Only for a moment. His hand, she saw, tanned, with long expressive fingers, trembled.

Then the day was there and across the street the tram lines glinted, hard as nails.

"I've lost my job," said Anna.

"I'm sorry."

"Oh, I don't mind. I like walking about. And I can easily find something."

"I thought," he said, "you might be an actress. Or a dancer."

Anna was amused, pleased. "Oh, no." These occupations had always seemed to her to require talent.

"You move so gracefully." he said. He blushed again.

Anna took his arm, and they walked down the street, and went to where the tram was already rolling towards them, separating as a knife.

But Anna got on the tram with him.

He didn't remonstrate or comment. He paid their fare and they sat together, near the back. Now the hat, tilted for utterly hopeless concealment, did manage to conceal his face from her. She wanted quietly to push the hat up. They spoke desultorily now, the words awkward. People might hear.

She wondered where they were going.

They got out in a sun-drenched rope of street, and then there were houses, stacked together like cards, and a door was open on a space and a stair.

"I live here," he said.

Anna was nonplussed, she couldn't quite see why. They had gone so far and so fast, and all at this hesitant, leisurely, halting pace.

Of course, she had gone directly with men to their rooms and lain down on their floors and beds with them. But those encounters were not this one.

"I'd love a glass of wine," Anna said, for there was a café she could see, with tables.

"I have some wine," he said, "in my room." He would not look at her, and now the left side of his face was stone white, like marble and the dead in books.

"Yes," said Anna.

They went up the stairs, and she wondered what she would see, and thought she had been unwise again. But the sun smashed through the narrow windows on to the treads of the stairs, and a clean threadbare carpet, and she could smell geraniums and furniture oil, coffee, and her own powder roused by the heat.

His room was very bare, with a table and some chairs, a cupboard, one cabinet without doors, full of books, a bed behind a curtain - a white curtain, like the white curtains at the windows. There was a wash-stand, and in cool water, the bottle of yellow wine. And on the table, a bowl of dark pink fruit that she did not identify for a long while as peaches, they seemed so curious, and new.

"Do you always have wine? How civilised."

"No. It was for you. I knew - I'd meet you."

Her heart slowed until she thought it had stopped. But it had been gathering itself for a leap.

"Oh, how?"

"I don't know."

"I saw you yesterday," she said, "in the café by the gardens."

"Perhaps it's that, then. I saw you too, and didn't know."

"You mean, you didn't remember me."

"No. I mean... It wasn't you, yesterday."

Anna laughed. She understood just what he meant, without understanding him at all.

They sat on the hard chairs at the table, and drank the wine. He had taken off his jacket, and the hat. She was fascinated by the pale shirt against his brown throat and hands. The fair hair whitening above the scarlet. Although, he kept his hand mostly over his right cheek.

She too took off her hat, her shoes.

They began to talk seriously, as if beginning on a very complicated meal, which it had taken them all their lives to prepare, and which must be approached with respect.

During this feast, of dialogue, she told of her childhood, her itinerant father hauling her from city to city. That she had never had the presence of a mother, but once, when she was twelve, was shown a most beautiful dead *embalmed* corpse, that she was informed had *been* her mother. And that she had not been able to make any connection between herself and it, though old women in black stood sobbing by her, urging her on to lament.

She mentioned borders crossed at night through woods and thorns. Olive groves, and a sea like turquoise. She explained her father had eventually disappeared. That she had made her way by herself.

(The peaches were from a hothouse, expensive. He cut them open, and they ate them, the syrup pouring back into the plates. And they licked the plates like cats, shamelessly.)

He told her, he had been intended to be a priest. "Because," he said, "of my face." When she seemed shocked, he laughed abruptly. Only God could put up with him, but then, God had done it to him in the first place. He passed from curtailed childhood to the loaf-thick walls, where he was beaten and starved, along with all the other boys. Here he grew up, seeing the village sometimes, on the side of the hill, where he had been born, far off as something viewed from the sky.

Then the priests had taken him aside. It seemed he wasn't fit for God either. The other boys were superstitious of him. The laity would be distressed by his appearance, when they should be fixing their minds on the Infinite.

Cast off, he too had made his way. He was clever with figures, that is, most people were so bad with them, his slight aptitude seemed like a talent.

The day had passed over like the amber sail of a windmill, altering the shadows in the room.

Blue scents now came through the half-parted windows.

"It's so late," he said. "You must go, Anna." And when she stared at him, stunned as if he had suddenly slapped her, he said, "It's been a wonderful day you've given me. I don't deserve it. I won't forget. But it's evening."

She said, her voice very little in the dusk, "But we could go out for a meal. I have lots of money saved. Let me pay for it. "

"No, Anna. Thank you. You said..."

"But I have. Really. My last employer left me something, you see."

"I'm glad. But I have enough. And anyway, I don't like brightly lit places, unless I must."

"Well, I can go to a shop and buy some food, some more wine..."

"Anna, Anna," he said.

There was a long silence.

Uncannily she heard the clang of a tram, down in the street, which all afternoon she must have done, and had not.

He said, "We have nowhere to go, Anna."

She knew his name, too, by this time. She used it. "Árpád," she said, "I'm not - it isn't - but I should like..."

Árpád rose. Against the window, his face was opalescently dark, like a jewel with one or two darker facets.

He went with her down to the street, and waited, his hat tilted, turned from the street lamps, for the tram to rush roaring up.

In the scuffle as other passengers got on, he pressed his cool mouth to her fingers.

"I will never forget you, darling."

As she sat on the tram, she saw raindrops had stained her skirt. There was no rain. Like the noise of the trams that afternoon, she had not heard the quiet sound of her own crying, until that moment.

As she walked Preguna, Anna saw an advertisement in the window of a fashionable shop. In Paris, or Athens, such a shop would be laughed at. Here it was quite important.

Anna went home, and manicured her nails, she put on her best summer dress, the sleeves of which she had had altered, like little gossamer wings. She combed her hair starkly and put on a hat of straw and net, and her reddest lipstick.

At the shop she was interviewed by another sharp woman, this one in a sharp dress of dark blue muslin.

Anna spoke succinctly, checking herself, watching every word. She dropped mentions of other cities. She had been working with a professor, a friend of her father's, on a historical work. But that was done now, and she was bored. It was either find something of interest to occupy her, or move on quickly to another place.

Probably the woman did not believe very many of these lies. She looked at Anna shrewdly.

"The assistant's post is filled. But we give a couple of little shows most weeks, for some of our clients, to display the nicer, more costly gowns. You have the right figure. You'd be surprised, the number of fifty-year-old women who think they'll look just the same, once they've seen a dress on a slim young girl."

So Anna was engaged as a model.

The work involved her only two or three afternoons a week, but she was paid much more than the professor had ever offered.

The shows were held in the large back premises of the shop, a big chamber of velvet chairs and a raised walk.

Here, with red lips and nails, powdered arms and face, Anna stalked in fine high-heeled shoes that had marquesite buckles or gilded bows, the tea gowns and evening dresses clinging to her slender new-moon curves. Not even knickers could be worn under such clothes, let alone a brassiere or garter-belt. The trick was to damp the body first with the wet sponge, next sliding the silk and satin home, so that it dried to the body like a second skin.

She discovered soon why she had been hired. The blue woman liked herself to look at slim young girls dressing or undressing, or simply sprawled, smoking, and bare but for their cosmetics. However Peepy, as the other three models called her behind her back, seldom touched and never propositioned.

"Oh, she's quite safe," said the brunette, "she lives with some old woman lover who's madly jealous. Peepy loves her, but likes to tickle her own fancy a bit with us." The redhead was coarsest. She would flaunt and tempt Peepy, approaching her to ask if Peepy would help with this dress or that, asking if she had a pimple on her bottom - yes, just there, it felt sore, or letting slip a strap to display one breast. Afterwards it was she who would call the woman other rather bestial names.

Anna did not mind Peepy. Even if Peepy had asked for more substantial favours, Anna would probably have granted them. She had usually granted them to men.

Perhaps it would have been a relief. Her mind was full of Árpád, her body was full of him. It fluttered and twanged, and sometimes, when she had not thought of him for half an hour, something would recall him to her, the hot sunlight falling on the backstairs of the shop, the tilt of a man's hat in the street, and her stomach would turn itself over, not quickly, but like a heavy, sinking wave. Alone, she would look at herself in a mirror, and she would think, *If only you could see me, just like this.*

Remembering things he had said, she heard his voice. He had a beautiful voice.

The idea of him passed over and over her, like the reflections of clouds. He was always with her.

She had never felt this way for any man. It was not desire, or not only desire. Sometimes she thought of him moving alone about Preguna, and her eyes stabbed with tears. Sometimes she felt a wild rage that echoed away through her brain, shouting his name, and she wanted to tie him to a post and beat him - but this image was a sexual one, and would soon resolve itself in arousal, and so to compassion and tenderness.

She tried to see how it must be for him. But she was only afraid he did not want her. So she looked into a mirror, turning her face to catch the light, widening her eyes until she was perfect, and then thinking, *If only he could see me as I am now.*

Now and then the other girls 'borrowed' dresses, for personal use outside the shop. They boasted of this to Anna. Presently she realised, from certain snide remarks, that they distrusted her, since she now knew their habit and had not succumbed as they had. This might lead to trouble. In another country, a petty pilferer had got Anna the sack because she had not wanted, or thought, of also companionably pilfering.

So Anna told the other girls she would like to wear the white silk gown one night, but she would wait until her friend took her somewhere suitable.

"Once she got a spot of red wine," said the brunette of the other blonde, "on one of the jackets. It was *moile* velvet. Guess what she did? She had the sewing girl sew a flower in gold beads over the stain. It cost a lot of money, but better than the cost of a whole jacket."

"And that woman from the cathedral street bought it," said the redhead, "and the silly cow said, Ooh look, what a cunning place to put a flower. It just *makes* the jacket."

Having staked a claim to the white dress, Anna began to study it, stroke it sometimes. She had modelled it twice, but it was very expensive, and cut only for the most svelte body. Women admired, but did not buy.

The white silk clung, then fell loosely below her knee to the ankle. Its low bosom described the breasts, the silk ending in two diamante straps. The back was even lower, where the diamante strands ran down to the waist, forming there a sparkling butterfly.

Anna, privately, had no notion of ever wearing the dress, except for the shows at the shop.

The last show, although Anna did not know it, was late on a thundery afternoon, the sky as low as a collapsed ceiling which seemed likely to fall down on the streets.

Anna put on the white silk dress in a cloud of powder, the sticky smells of women, their scent and clean sweat, in her nose.

Beyond the curtain, which the shop coyly put up between the models' entrance and the waiting customers, all the velvet chairs were full. The high buzz and squeaks of female voices. The fan whirring round and round, like a spider, in the roof.

Peepy sat very upright in a coal-dark dress in the front row. Beside her was another woman, much older, with a wonderful raddled face and huge eyes, ringed in kohl. She had brassy earrings like a gypsy's.

"Look, look," said the girls, "it's Peepy's old loveress. She's forced her way in."

At first nothing happened. The redhead, then the blondes (including Anna), then the brunette, emerged, displayed the shop's finery, and retreated.

The old lover - she might be seventy - sat crouched and baleful. Her mouth was stony, and her great eyes carved from ink and pain. She ceaselessly smoked; her cigarettes were brown and poked into a holder of cloudy jade. She consumed them as if she hated them and paid them out.

When Peepy got up to indicate some frill or accessory, the old lover glared at her.

Such hatred, such malevolence. Such absolute concentration.

Anna recognized a burning and devouring, awful, magnificent love.

Do I feel this - any of this - for him?

Yes - she thought - *yes* - and as she stepped out on the walk, now in the white silk dress, (which someone had apparently wanted to see), she raised her head like a fierce horse scenting battle. She wanted to run to him at once, to tear him open with her teeth and nails, to touch his heart, to drink his blood...

It was at this instant, as Anna was halfway along the walk, that the lover sprang from her seat. She pushed out into the space before the chairs, and turning, faced the audience of well-bred, wealthy women.

"I have seen enough. She is harlot. She is *faithless*. Honour - what is honour to her? We grow old. Even this one - this lily of white in her *skin* - she too - *she too* - Once I was this. I - better. But now I am nothing. Quick! To graveyard with me. *Harlot! Harlot!*"

Peepy had risen. The room was still as deafness, only the resonance of the maddened voice yet tolling in it like the clapper of a brazen bell.

The old lover wept. Black streamed down her face. She was the essence of a tragedy ancient as the world.

And Peepy, first white with shock, then flushed with shame, then everything forgotten, rushed to her and caught her in her arms, smothering her with kisses and cries before them all.

Anna, made drunk by their passion, and no longer noticed by anyone, went briskly back along the walk.

Even the girls took no note, and the women who sewed were crowding to the front to see.

Anna seized her bag, her clothes. She flung over herself the nearest thing, like a dust-sheet, and half ran from the shop by its back way.

It was about six o'clock.

Anna sat on the tram, clutching her bundle, wrapped in the black silk evening cloak, the white silk glimpsing under it, the silver shoes, a diamanté clip in her hair, her stockings invisibly held by white garters, and not a stitch otherwise on her.

She was glanced at.

During the carnival, she had heard, here in Preguna, they wore evening-dress, and masks, and other means of disguise and facial decoration. But Carnival was not yet.

When she reached the street like a rope, a storm had begun.

She left the tram and walked through space, the wind whipping the black cloak. Thunder tumbled like masonry from clouds of purple plaster, and dust spun.

Everything was in motion. The thunder chanted in her blood.

She could not decide which was his lodging house. How stupid. Then she saw the white curtains blowing behind a half-opened window.

Perhaps he wasn't here. Had gone away for a year.

Anna opened the outer door, and climbed up the stairs, which now were black, or spirited by lightning. The rain began in a burst of shattered glass.

I shall never be old, thought Anna. *I can't imagine I will. Something will happen to me, before then.*

This buoyed her up.

She reached the landing, and the door. She stood there.

Thunder crashed. The rain smashed. Light and shade raced over and through her. The house might collapse, and she would not have touched him.

She beat on the door insanely, calling.

It was flung open.

He was there, in shirt-sleeves. How tall he was. His eyes so luminous. The cannonade of the thunder made it seem Preguna was under siege.

"Anna..."

In the war zone of life she cried desperately: "I've lost everything! I stole this dress! I'm a thief! I've nowhere to go!"

Árpád took her hand, and led her gently in through the door, to the blown and storm-tossed room beyond.

Chapter Five: A Reasonable Attempt

The morning after she had seen the Basulte male making love to, or raping, a female servant in the roof conservatory, Anna got up early, about seven, before any of them arrived in her room.

She dressed in the plain chic dress from Paris, and filled her largest handbag with anything she had left, that was of use.

Then she put on her coat and hat, and the galoshes which had somehow been abandoned here following the wet walk with Raoul.

She had some money, in English currency, which Raoul had given her idly, on their reaching the country. It had never, of course, been utilised. Anna had no idea if it would be enough, but she thought so, these substantial crackling papers, and the bright burnished coins.

She descended through the house, prepared to say that she was going for a 'turn about the gardens', a phrase she had found in a book.

Only two of the maids passed her, eyes down, bobbing and cowering, scuttling on.

Because she could not recall the way to the front of the house, she went down to the orangery and the salon, from which a passage led away to the storage and gun rooms, the route Raoul had taken her.

At eight, the men would use the breakfast room, but that was somewhere across the house. The women took their breakfast in bed. Unless, for some reason Raoul had also lied about this.

But no one was about, though the salon curtains had been folded back, and a maid was kneeling in the fireplace, clearing up the evening fire.

The door to the gun room stood ajar, smelling of gun lubricant and tinders.

A mouse - or perhaps a maid, reduced to Lilliputian size - scuttled by behind the wall.

Outside, and down the damp mossy steps, Anna surveyed the sea of mud that was the path up and around to the drive.

A cedar, frosted blue, towered on a lawn. There was a walled kitchen garden. An elderly man with a wheelbarrow full of cabbage toiled along, and seeing her, bowed his head, and touched his brow with one arthritic claw.

But the rain only sparkled, shed like dew, on every blade and leaf. The far-off hills seemed cut by a knife. The sky was clear, pure as glass. The sun shone, young and pale, flashing among the Basulte trees.

As she was walking through the park in the morning sunshine, a rider on a black horse went galloping by, so near she felt the heat, and off among the historic oak trees.

If he saw her she couldn't have said. It was Raoul, probably. She thought it was. Behind him sat Lilith Lizard, her sandy hair flying free, her goat eyes narrowed.

She was clinging to Raoul, her face pressed into his back. Her expression, but for the narrowed eyes, was unfathomable.

Actually, Anna might have been invisible. Maybe she was. Though the mud of their going had lightly splashed her coat, she had entered another universe.

His brother - William? - had said Raoul had a woman here.

It didn't matter now. Anna was leaving.

She had not cared anything for Raoul. It had been an error. But she always made mistakes. Her forté.

To proceed, she had thought she must go to the village. Here she might be able to persuade someone to take her to the nearest town or station. She had seen no cars she could recollect in the village. She might have to ride on a cart, or something like that. Elsewhere she had done this, from time to time, over the long white dusty roads, through groves of orange trees and figs and apples. In another life, the past.

Anna believed she had memorized, inadvertently, the way Raoul had led her to the village.

But soon she was lost, as in the Basulte house.

Brilliant sunlight too, seemed to change things. There were more colours; birds sang or squeaked, and butterflies danced on the green stalks of the fields.

In one of the lanes, an old brown man came stooping out of a field, with a lean tan dog on a piece of string. When he saw her, the man touched his cap, and made the bowing motion. But his back was bent anyway, perhaps from decades of such ghastly grovelling.

The dog only stared, then lifted its leg against the stile.

"The village," said Anna, "is it...?"

"Yooum Mus Animal," said the old man.

Anna contemplated this version of her name: Anna Moll, Miss Animal.

"Yooum gum frotha ouse."

"Oh... yes. A walk. The village."

"I knows," said the ancient man, "byee hair."

"Do you know the way?" Anna said.

The old man began to crawl along the lane, talking to her, with the dog trotting at his side. Did this mean the man was taking her to the village?

"Thold sunce out," said the old man.

"Yes," said Anna.

"Byar oll sumba."

Anna kept silent.

The chestnut trees overhung the lane, nettles and wild parsley flourished. The dog constantly snuffed things and made water over them. The pace of the old slow man allowed ample space for that. The man talked on and on, now mostly incomprehensibly.

Anna wanted to run away.

"Is the village this way? Down there?" she asked in the end.

The old man lifted his old face to the old sun. She had seen such faces on peasants everywhere. Baked so hard, a hundred wrinkles worked in leather. He looked one hundred, and might be sixty-five.

Running downhill, the lane grew narrow. Cows stood motionless yet with mechanically swishing tails. A small wood enveloped the road.

From shadow, yesterday's rain dripped, sprinkling lights. The dog shook itself.

The old man had not answered any of her questions, that was, her repeated question, but as they left the wood, the lane turned, and a rundown cottage appeared, with burnt green paint and a rickety water-butt.

"Here are," said the old man. He moved through the broken fence, and by the door let the dog free of the string. "G'dee, Mus Animal." The door shut. The dog bolted into a hedge.

Deserted on the track, Anna frowned. She wanted to shout invective after the man, but really it wasn't his fault, she supposed.

Dismally she went on down the lane, and found, beyond the next bank of trees, the village was before her, spangled in the sun, all its doors and flowers open wide.

Anna paused, undecided. There were women about mostly, with baskets, or pegging out washing in their little grassy yards, where roses grew in hearts of blood.

But the first woman glanced at Anna, and then, strangely, quickly away.

Anna crossed to the low wall. "Excuse me, please..."

The woman dropped a sort of curtsy, not quite the house bob, scattered her clothes pegs and trotted away indoors, Across the gardens, the width of the village street from her, was the public house, with its sign of the knight and the dainty dragon.

Anna went there.

The interior was now not so dark, sunlit from the door and the little pebbly windows. Red blooms stood in pots, and there were brown jugs with round hips gathered on the counter. The ceiling was low, and a bird cage hung from the beams, without a bird.

The room was full of men, Anna saw, huge brown men. Some smoked pipes, and most drank glasses of beer, and there were plates of bread and ham and cheese, and dishes of yellow mustard and jars of magenta pickles.

Over all floated a clock, with its hands at eleven.

Had she been so long wandering about? How could that be? Yet it had *seemed* several hours, at least.

There was only one woman in the bar-room, but for

herself, Mrs Izzard-Lizard, who leaned on the counter with her fat tawny arms. She wore over her dress a blue pinafore dotted with sprigs of flowers. Her eyes were today the colour of water in which such flowers might have died.

"G'dee. Muz," said Mrs Izzard, showing her selected teeth. "Can I gee a drink?"

"Thank you," said Anna. She felt the eyes of the giants on her fragile back, piercing through her too-hot coat.

Mrs Izzard did not ask what Anna would have, and Anna was quite glad. She thought there would be nothing but beer or strong ale, for women were not entitled to drink here. But after all there were some large gleaming bottles set to one side and from one of these a colourless fluid was poured, into a long-stemmed glass.

This was placed before Anna, but when the woman specified money, Anna could not understand the sum. She put one of the crackling notes on the counter.

"Thassa take all my till, my dearie," said Mrs Izzard. "But Mas Rarl issa sum."

She took the note and put it away, and brought back to Anna a cupped palm of overflowing shining coins.

"You gwon fur the ladies' perlor," said Mrs Izzard, and coming out from the counter by means of a flap, showed Anna into a small back room.

Here was a single table, with a crocheted mat, and three chairs upholstered in something like sackcloth. A vase without anything in it stood on the windowsill, where lay also an exquisite dead moth with tissue wings. There was a painting on the wall of a girl child in old-fashioned dress, and with a pig's face.

Mrs Izzard put down a brown jug, which was filled

with water.

Anna sipped her drink. It might be gin. Raoul had bought her a gin at a station. This was very acid, metallic.

"I have to go up to London," said Anna, speaking slowly and distinctly. "Would someone drive me to the nearest station? I shall be happy to pay, of course."

"No stazn a males," said Mrs Izzard. She smiled her teeth. When she did this, each time Anna felt a need to count them. "Twod be a longold drav."

"But I must," said Anna.

She thought, *Oh of course I can't escape. They won't let me go.* But that was totally unreasonable.

Mrs Izzard spoke with mild decision. "You drink your glaz, Muz, anile seef uny willin. You set."

Anna said quickly, "Five pounds."

She guessed this was a ridiculous amount, but Mrs Izzard smiled now with her mouth *shut*, so Anna couldn't count.

"Ull see. You set. Jusset, beyeezy."

She went out, and Anna had another mouthful of the gin, which stung her like a serpent.

The parlour was hot. Presently she undid her coat. She felt inadequate and silly, fleeing in fear from the sinister mansion, like a heroine. Anna was not a heroine.

She could hear the murmur of the giants' voices, the clink of glasses. Sunlight bubbled, trilled.

The poor moth. It must have been shut in here and died, dashing itself fruitlessly at the window.

Anna's head drooped. Her ears sang like the sea. She shut her eyes, only for a moment.

When she opened her eyes, she was in bed. She had the impression the bed, too, was in a box. A hot box.

Everything was greyish-brown, but for one slab of latening apricot light. For some reason, although this was not the same, she was reminded of the hospital at Preguna. She was swathed in a cotton nightdress.

The next time her eyes opened, which now they seemed to do without her volition, a bloated vulpine face drifted from the ruddy gloom.

"Yuad a litt bid of a turn, my dearie. Nodda fret."

Anna knew she was indeed a prisoner. (There had been another one, below, hadn't there, in the parlour, lying dead.)

She pushed her hand - it looked so frail and white - up over the tons of heavy quilt. The diamond Raoul had bought for her glimmered cool.

"Do - you - want this?"

"Wun that, my dearie? Never."

"Take it, please. It's quite valuable. I must get to..." Where was it? Anna felt panic rise. She remembered. "To London."

"Butta dunt wan her, Muz Animal. Tes only a bidda glass."

Chapter Six: Entering Through Doors

Returning was not like the arrival. Not at all.

It was night, for one thing, or rather, earliest morning, and everything was black but for the headlamps of the creaking old car. The car was not up to the short journey from the village to the house. It stopped two or three times. The car did not want to take Anna back.

In the rear seat, wrapped up in a rug, Anna saw the lanes go by. Starlight thin as wires poked into the fields. When they entered the gate she must have made a little sound for the huge man who sat beside her, Mr Lizard (Izzard) patted her hand. "Umos theer."

Anna didn't want to be theer.

But presently theer she was.

The park was black and from the black rose the black house, without a single light anywhere that could be seen.

Anna thought of prisoners delivered to jails such as the Conciergerie, in dead of night.

The car toiled round the drive, and then off through another line of trees, and so into the yard of a stable which Anna had not encountered until then.

They helped her out, the driver and Mr Lizard, and she believed they were going to bed her down in one of the stalls, where she could hear the horses stirring vaguely, so vaguely she wondered if they were horses at all, and not some other animal species, something more eccentric, bulls perhaps, or tigers.

Then there was a lamp and a side door, and a

woman, two women, were taking her in, like a precious parcel.

When the door shut, the men and the night were outside. The lamp went ahead, and one woman only guided her. Anna's body seemed too large for her, and lacking feeling. She was somewhere in the centre of it, bumped about like a bottle on a river. There were stairs. So many stairs... Often they had to stop and wait for her.

Another door. She was assisted inside, and here was another bed, not a Basulte bed, narrow, with an iron frame. She was being helped to lie down, as if she did not know how to. And she didn't.

A bank of lumpen pillows cradled her head. Good heavens, they were undressing her. Deft impersonal hands. Again, she remembered the hospital.

As the new coarse nightdress was eased over her, and the quilts pulled up, and the stone sausage with hot-water rolled against her feet, she thought that of course, they had drugged her in the pub.

Things faded.

"Thas mur cumvy," said one of the women.

It was. How unsuitable.

Anna moved, disorganized, about in dreams. She knew that Árpád had left her. They had been walking along a street and between one sentence and the next, he was gone. She understood unalterably that she had caused this, done something wrong, to offend or hurt him, and he had previously warned her, if she did this thing, he would go. And she had not meant to do it, but she had done it. It was inexorable.

His omission was like something added rather than lost, an aching leaden burden in her stomach, her belly.

But while she felt it, while it underlay everything, she

had other dreams. That she was on a train or in an apartment, or in a market. The buildings were very tall, of monstrous architecture and extreme sculptural decoration. Where landscape was glimpsed, it stretched for hundreds of miles, to ponderous horizons under galleons of cloud.

These dreams were exhausting. She woke, trembling with the fatigue of them.

A decanter of water and a glass were on the table. She had to drink the water, even if they had put something in it. She drank the decanter dry.

Then she slept again, and the enervating dreams went on and on. Until she woke, and now there was a dark whiteness of deadish light, and the decanter had been refilled and she drank it dry again.

The water had a dusty taste.

Inside her, the leaden feeling of loss, like a stone forced into her womb, had gone away, but there remained a black residue, a pain that did not hurt.

Anna lay back. She wanted someone to come and make her wake up, because the dreams were so tiresome and wore her out. She always had to do something in them, go somewhere, achieve something. But no sooner had she managed the task, than it was all to do again. Like the labours in Hell.

Yet, now she slept dreamlessly, a clear blue sleep. And waking, she was able to sit up in the bed, then get out of it.

She no longer felt drugged, but she was puzzled, and uneasy, naturally.

This room was very, very small. The narrow single bed took up most of the space. Fusty curtains covered the window, and when she pulled them wide, outside was a brick wall with a drainpipe. Rain was falling again, very soft and fine.

To her surprise, Anna saw her clothes were on a chair. Then she saw they were other clothes. Rather a long black belted dress, some under things, plainer than the lingerie Raoul had bought her. The shoes were also different, not very nice, although when she put them on they fitted perfectly. Her bag lay under the chair.

There were a jug of cold water and a basin, a bit of soap in a dish and a thin towel. Anna washed. She opened her bag.

Surprising her, her passport was still there. And some of her toiletries emerged, an old medicine bottle, the essentials. But of her make-up, only her powder showed itself.

Things had been stolen, obviously - confiscated. Her brain was beginning to wake now, after her body, and she was trying to reason. She had been put in this odd room out of the way. She would have to be circumspect, perhaps seem a little dazed. Certainly not annoyed or primed for conflict.

She had learned one thing. The village possessed the ramshackle car. She had constantly seen people drive cars. Perhaps she could do it. Failing that, she would simply have to walk. By-passing the village, evidently, keeping on just like someone in a story, until she reached some other more distant place, where help was to be had.

Anna was not frightened. She felt more exasperated. It was always possible to evade capture. She knew this quite well. How often had she seen her father, and others, do it? Had done it quite adequately herself, in the past.

But she would need to be careful. If she were questioned about her first escape, she would just say she had become confused. No, she hadn't said *she* wanted to go to London. She had said she and *Raoul* would be going there, sometime. She would accuse no one of drugging her - she must have fainted: the long walk when she had got lost, the sudden hot day.

When she had dressed and combed her hair and powdered her face, Anna tried the door. In the moment of doing this, she wondered if it would be locked. But the door opened normally, and outside was a corridor narrow as the iron bed.

Where was she? The corridor was painted the colour of the porridge the Basultes sometimes consumed, Raoul had said, at breakfast - the porridge offered her in English station hotels, and refused.

There were two doors, both of which gave on tiny rooms like the one she had been put into.

At the end of the corridor was a biggish open space, or perhaps only seeming big by comparison, where trunks and boxes stood. The ceiling of rafters sloped to one side, as she thought the ceiling had done in the room. There were two windows.

Anna looked out.

Far below, lawns, beeches, the river. The hills were smeared into rain mist, a running water-colour.

Across the space, another corridor tunnelled away. But there was also a large latched door, and when she undid it, she gazed down into the well of a grim lean staircase, very dark, descending and descending through the house. For up here, she had slept among the attics, where the servants slept.

On the mystic down-leading staircase there came occasional landings. When she tried the doors, they were locked. She had no choice but to continue her descent.

The stair ended in an annexe with several doors and a long window, with curtains of a sort of material she had seen in cheap hotels.

One of the doors became a gap and the housekeeper called Mrs Pin stepped smartly out, like a cuckoo springing from a clock at the appointed hour.

"There you are, Annie," said Mrs Pin.

Anna looked at her.

"You must be quite hungry," said Mrs Pin, briskly. In a moment her chorus-girl side would get the better of her, she would rip off her long skirt and kick up fishnet legs, smiling yellow to the theatre balcony. "Go along there, and straight down."

Anna said, "Do you mean to the kitchen?"

"Yes, Annie. That's right."

After all, a welter of fear tossed up through Anna. What should she do? Nothing - nothing. She reined herself in quickly.

"Very well."

Mrs Pin said, "Don't be alarmed. They expect you."

"Do they?"

"You've nothing to worry about," said Mrs Pin.

She stood sentinel, as Anna went across the room, chose the proper door, and pushed through and down again, down.

She was being punished. That must be it. They were a law to themselves, and she a vagabond, and they might do what they liked, so they had cast her below.

She was not to be Raoul's wife. (She had come to suspect that anyway, rather swiftly.) She was to dwell among the 'dogs' - the servants.

Her dress was black. Would the apron and cap come

next?

Anna hesitated on the last stair. She was truly frightened. Less than the chaos of this situation, it was the *servants* she feared. She could hear them now behind the final door. They were laughing, perhaps in anticipation, loudly and coarsely, and banging things - probably pans - in what sounded like the prologue to a war dance.

Even their language was alien to her. And besides, they had had to wait as slaves on her. What revenge would they take?

She must not protest. She must be, as so often, accommodating. Give in and so invite no violence. Escape was still always achievable, providing she were extremely careful. She had not realised before, not believed her own impulse, that the Basultes were creatures out of a myth, something horrible. However, now she knew.

She bowed her head, and went in through the door, slinking and a little abject, not to invite the viciousness of this other species.

Anna remembered the great kitchen from her compulsory Sunday visit, brought by the woman, Raoul's Mother. It had been so clean, immaculate. The linoleum still damp, windows bright, the bowl of fruit and the flowers. Everyone had lined up, women and men, as if to be chastised.

What time of day was it now? The universal rain-twilight had made it difficult to tell. Also afternoon, perhaps.

The three long tables were not scrubbed, nor bare. Pots and bowls lay over them, and pans of copper and iron. These were dirty, and a smell rose from them of boiled vegetable matter, fish and cheese. The ovens too were crowded by debris. The floor was splashed, and greasy.

Two gaunt cruel-looking cats were lapping from a big dish of gravy. A large, freshly-dead rat lay stiffening nearby. Presumably they had killed it and been rewarded.

A fire burned, and a maid was toasting at it platefuls of buns, piling them high so that sometimes some fell off on to the floor. At last one of the cats took note. It rushed and seized half a bun and bounded away. From somewhere in the kitchen an arm was raised. An item of crockery, thrown at the cat, missed it, and smashed to pieces.

At this, the collective coarse wild laughter rose again. Anna looked at them, for they had not turned to look at her. Like the tables, the kitchen was crowded. It was hot and ill-smelling, and lightnings went over it from disturbed cutlery and plates. Women sat, as Anna had seen them in the summer doorways of houses elsewhere, their legs spread wide, hands busy with darning and sewing.

No bonnets were worn. The thick rich filthy-looking hair spilled from its knots and pins. Their aprons, if on, were patterned with stains. Some were barefoot on the greasy linoleum.

One fed a baby from her breast, there in the middle of the frowsy blowsy scene. Among the farms or slums of Europe this would not seem amiss, but here it was a dissolute image, augmented soon, for the girl - she was about fourteen - took from the table a bottle of some dark alcohol, and put it first to her mouth, next tipped it over her nipple. It would keep the child quiet.

Anna felt a disturbed flash of pity. But it wasn't wise

to pity these people. She must only respect them, and be wary.

"Whussat?" a voice shouted.

Anna knew this alarm heralded her entry.

She saw the cook called Ox propped in a gargantuan chair. Her stockinged feet, misshaped by bunions, were on a footstool. Her hair too was half unpinned, and her face incredibly like red cabbage. There was a tankard in her hand, which a boy now hurried to fill up, aslosh, with beer.

"Here's our Unny," said the cook.

What world had she come to? Downwards - it must be the Inferno.

Anna confronted the cook, and all the faces turning now to her, even the fur-sketched face of the cat with its beard of gravy.

And Anna bowed, as she had seen them do, to the ones who were, just, their superiors.

"Cummer," said the cook. "You sittun by me, Unny."

Was this a welcome?

Anna walked through the room, through its dense veils of staring and heat, the flicker of fire and rain on windows.

The cook patted her hand. "God gul."

A maid, her buttons undone, grinning, brought Anna a bun, and buttered it before her. Poured chocolate-coloured tea from the big black pot.

Anna was hungry. She ate with care. The cook said to her, soft as a bee, "You'll likun bedder here."

And the maid, her breasts white-bulging in her undone bodice, leaning over Anna with the cup of tea, remarked, "Yoon ourn now."

When he had led her in, and closed the door, Árpád put Anna into a chair she did not recall. He had taken the cloak from her, or it had fallen. He brought her a glass of something which she thought was wine, but it was water.

The storm vented a burst of light, and this apparently happened inside the glass, and Anna dropped it, thinking the glass had shattered.

"It's all right. Be calm, dearest. You stole this dress? I'll buy it for you. You can say it was a mistake."

"Would you? Would you?"

"Why did you take it?"

"I don't know. Yes, I do. To come to you."

He shook his head.

The storm howled and exploded; it was like the end of the world, and so made all things permissible.

Anna left the chair. She fell at his feet and clasped his knees. She laid her cheek against his thigh. "Don't send me away."

"Oh Anna."

But he was utterly still, and then she got up and put her bare arms round his neck, and pressed her mouth against his fine-made lips. He let her kiss him, and then, as if remembering, began to kiss in turn. But he was very gentle, as though at any moment she would realise she had lost her mind and what she was doing, and leap away, spitting and cursing him. In his kiss there was all of that, and a terrible *unspeakable* forgiveness for when she did.

Anna drew back. "I love you."

"Dear Anna."

"I love you, Árpád."

He too drew away from her, quietly. At first he half turned, hiding the right side of his face which, anyway, in the gusting night and conflagration of the storm, she could barely see. Then he turned back, and his eyes met hers. He looked deeply into her brain. After all, she had never seen a gaze more steady. Or less kind.

"You see, darling Anna, there are only two races among humanity. Those that have power, and those that haven't any power. It may come from anything, the power. From money, from good looks, or cleverness - from normalcy, even. But to be powerless is to lack these things, or most, or even *some* of these things."

His eyes were black, yet when the lightning came, chrome-blue like the sea.

"Anna, the race that has the power - these people are gods. Like you, Anna - did you know you were a pale goddess? Like you. But those who lack this power are only *dogs*. The *dogs*, Anna, who must worship and serve the gods. Anna, I don't want to be your dog."

She edged the glittering diamanté straps from her shoulders, and pushed down the dress to her waist. A primitive gesture, like the making of fire. He stared at her breasts. Perhaps he had never seen...

Inside her, all of her spun, fragmented between terror and joy, grief and desire.

She raised her arms again and caressed his face, stroking with her fingers both sides of it, the tanned and the carnelian side. Had she been blind, she could have told no difference. But lightning dazzled, and his face *was* like the face of a god, two images in one, blood and golden, ice and fire, silence and red music.

He kissed now as other men had. His hands slid warm on the bare skin of her back.

She knew there would never be another, knew they had grown together. Now the bark of a tree would enclose them, arched into each other's bodies, their souls burnt through flesh and bone, adhering in one eternal molten gasp.

He had never made love to a woman before. She knew this now, knew he must learn her. He was so gradual. He *felt* his way across her, through her. Yet he made so sure of her that she broke around him in a whirlpool as soon as he entered her. And as he lost control himself, they were tumbled out down the tumult of the dark.

In the seconds after, she was afraid he would thank her. She would do almost anything to prevent it. She blazed with preparatory shame. But he didn't thank her. He lay beside her unspeaking for a long while, as the storm melted, its purpose accomplished, for everything had conspired to render him to her. Then he began again to make love to her, unspeaking still. Unspeaking. They did not speak at all.

The first morning, she was frightened a long while. Later, they had a conversation about this.

"I thought you'd send me away," Anna said.

"I thought you would go away."

"But I love you so much. Why would I go?"

"Anna, you're like a child. Why do you think?"

"But you knew I wasn't drunk - or quite mad..."

"There might have been some other reason."

"Yes," she said, "but I told you. I never belonged with anyone else."

They discussed what was to be done about the dress. He would arrange it, by letter. He had some money put by. She protested; she would return the dress. But he didn't want that. She looked so lovely in the dress, and then when she emerged partly from it, like the butterfly from a cocoon of whiteness.

Time had stopped, and Anna did not care what they did, at first. But then they made changes to the room, and Anna's few possessions came into the room. There began to be bowls of marigolds, and poppies, and convolvulus, bottles of wine, more books stacked here and there, an oriental wind-chime that rang when the curtains blew, cushions on the bed.

After the dress had been bought, she continued a while at the dress shop, but the girls asked her things, and she was afraid to speak. It was like trying to prevent herself weeping or shrieking, her need to pour it all forth. And she didn't want to say a word. She drifted away, and so left.

She wasn't bored in their room, even when he was out, attending to his intelligent book-keeping. She dozed and read, or she went out and shopped, bringing back fresh flowers and bunches of herbs, bread, sausage, cheese and coffee, fruit and cake, tall candles banded with gold.

Though it was not always possible, he preferred to go out very early, before much light came, and to return in the twilight. She argued with nothing. They didn't talk about it. When they went out together, it was by night, to dim-lit places along some canal, to gardens with arbours of shadow.

Preguna under the moon was made of a forest of darkness, and white poured milk.

He bought her things, a little silver ring with an apple-green jewel, a clip for her hair. (And she bought him a tie coloured like a snake.) She must have realised he was not poor. But it would have made no difference, surely, immaterial almost. Things were meant to be as they were. He and she could not have avoided this.

Had there been happy eras in the past? She seemed to see there only always movement, and gaudy fleeting acted improvisations. Here in the shadows, far from that garish stage, timelessly they danced their subtle, perfect measure.

It was inexplicable. Even later, desperately looking back, she could make no sense of it. Their love had been like the most natural thing, soon taken for granted utterly, lived out because there was nothing else that might be done. Like youth. Like life itself.

Chapter Seven: Among the Pack of Dogs or Cards

As a child, often borne randomly and without preparation into some place, where she did not know the language of the people, Anna would be puzzled days and weeks. She was like a deaf person, for all the use she got from the chattering all around. Then abruptly some crystal membrane would tear wide. Suddenly she could understand. And in her head the new language came alive; needing no translation. Thoughts and visions available instantaneously as words.

It was rather like this with the dialect of the Basulte servants. In a few days of hearing only their voices her ignorance ceased. Then she heard them speak in English for the first time. Mimicking, as she had done since childhood, the alien sounds, she was also able to speak back to them in their own tongue.

"Oor kite unoor uz nay, enum, Unny?" That is, "You're quite one of us now, aren't you, Annie?"

This accolade from one of the kitchen maids. Anna responded with a smile that she was glad to be.

(She had seen her father ingratiate himself with the most loathsome and dangerous people. It was a game which had fascinated him, and she never witnessed him lose it, no, not once. Almost, it seemed to her, he sought out madmen, drunks and felons, in order to play with them and to win. He compared mankind to a pack of cards - there the joker, there the king or the jack, or the well-dressed queen - who might be a whore (hearts) or a rich man's mistress (diamonds). The secret however was

109

to play not *with* but with*in* the pack. They must never sense manipulation. You must believe utterly, while with them, what you did and said.

She had watched him with a politician once, a type he detested and held in contempt. But her father seemed gradually to fall in love with the man, admire him, even to be a little bewildered at his own change of heart.

And the politician was subtly flattered, and so betrayed confidences, and lent her father a large sum of money, which, naturally, was used instantly to fly the country.)

The servants didn't ask her to do very much. She peeled a few vegetables, stirred cakes and put cherries on to them. Now and then she offered to wash pans and dishes, or take bread from the ovens. They allowed this. Once the cook handed her an apron to sew, but Anna sewed badly, in uneven stitches. Then they mocked her, but only amused, patronisingly, with no hint of menace, and someone else finished the apron, which they then gave her.

Nor was this apron like theirs. It was the palest blue, with a pocket and an edging of lace. (And no one had taken her ring.)

She was like a child of the Family, allowed to act out Being of Help in the Kitchen.

They would sit and talk to her too, at the table. Their histories amazed her, they were so devoid of anything, and yet mattered so much, for the one who told his or her story was its hero.

They were all intrinsically feral and cruel. They laughed as if at a circus over a crippled rabbit, before breaking its neck for the pot. They smashed mice in the trap with a poker, discussing other things as they did it.

While from each other's ills, a bleeding chilblain, an agony of toothache, they fashioned hearty jokes.

Among the pack, Anna made certain to look at everything that occurred, or was perpetrated, through their eyes. They could do no wrong, and she treated them with respect and interest, showing the willingness to be taught.

The kitchen was hell, the centre of their demonism, the *hub*, but as they spread out through the house, like flies, they took their pandemonium with them. And they took Anna with them too, to see and learn, acquiesce and render praise.

Along with their tongue, she discovered from herself a new laugh, just like theirs, sly or brash - animal.

Out in the house, invisibly, they *did* things.

That is, things not their work. Or perhaps it *was* their work. Weren't they creatures of misrule - the Enemy? Dogs who fawned, but had hidden teeth.

In the bedrooms first, they showed her how they made the beds.

It was done carefully and quickly, the sheets shaken, the pillows plumped. And then, deep down, a tiny bit of something, gently laid. What was it?

"From a nettle," said the girls. They smiled and nodded at Anna. One explained it would chafe and sting, but, so small, would not be found. They did not do it every time, of course. Now and then. In different beds. This was the Basulte Father's room. He often didn't use it, preferring the couch in his study. Once they had sprinkled fine pepper there and he sneezed and hawked for hours. But that was a treat, not for everyday.

Later they took Anna back into the apartment of Margaret Lilian, and here each one pulled a hair from her own head. They coiled these together. "May it wrap round your guts," they said to the sheets and the hairs. They giggled, pleased, and pulled up the covers. It was a charm for ill, some old up-country thing.

All over the house they put their maledictions, if nothing else, soft and secret, nothing too much, nothing that could really be found, or if found, mean anything.

They showed her later, these ones, others, the servants who could write wrote little quick curses - *May you get a canker, May you shoot blood* - on paper scraps, and then burnt them lovingly in a candle, and the maids scattered the ash laughing between the blanket and the mattress, or behind a curtain, a basin.

They wrote in clear spit on woodwork *Take sick* and *Itch with no easing.*

They spat white phlegm or smeared earwax in the baths, after cleaning, and rubbed it in like polish.

Sometimes they ran, round and round on the carpets, like hares, whispering, almost bursting with a ribald hatred so pure and primordial it seemed to chime. *Foam and rave, drop in a grave,* they sang. Children's games.

And Anna looked on wondering, and did not shrink, and clapped her hands, looking through their eyes. These poor offended slaves, worthy of so much better than slavery. (Slaves must always have done such things.)

She too had lain in water and bath-salts and wax and gobbings, and slept in a cancer-wished bed... that one black hair - not Raoul's, not William's. Whose? This girl? That one?

If there was a pimple, its gleanings were dabbed inside the newly-burnished shoes, the stocking drawer.

There were other things they had devised.

She saw it on the second day she was with them.

There had been a rat in the trap. And the cook was making a large meat pie.

Under the golden crust, among the wholesome body parts of cows, *this* too.

"Oh, Madam loves her pie, she does," said Mrs Ox, contentedly.

They spat into the pots of tea, the casseroles and sauces, tea-cakes and meringues.

The gardener brought them worms. Once a woman slunk in from the village. A neighbour had given birth and the midwife retained some debris.

Anna laughed merrily, and then went out to the privy in the yard. She vomited as she had her first night with Raoul, though more quickly. They might have wanted...

She had eaten such dishes.

Going back, they told her she was pasty - pale - and watched her, grinning, thrilled, waiting. She owned up to her weakness. How strong *they* were to handle such things. She said she wished she had had the courage to do it.

"That old Raoul treated you like a bitch," said one of the girls.

Anna saw none of the Basultes. She was led by back-ways, hidden arteries, about their house. At night she slept now in the attics in a room of three beds. Only one other was filled. "That one's Lily's," said this other girl.

When the first Sunday came, Anna wondered if Madam would come down to the kitchen to inspect it, and if so how they would clean it to the perfection she had formerly seen. For the den was Hell, and a den of vice, which reminded her always of the horrors of Hogarth. Eternally pans unwashed on tables, swept off to the floors that the pack might themselves eat. Beer bottles, the shed fur of cats, the cats' fleas, from which Anna now had bites, both cats' and fleas', of her own.

As the fire burned and the heat rose, she sat among them and they petted her. The men petted her as they did the other girls, a kiss slapped on a cheek, a swift fondle of breast or thigh - never worse. (And sometimes they would even ask: "May I try a bit of titty?") The girls brushed her hair, and she theirs. Mutual grooming among the pack.

In fact, Madam never came down. It seemed that had been some test of Anna, not the staff.

Despite their early start, they all sat up late. The cook loomed huge in her chair, drinking gin and beer.

They sang songs full of naive sweetness. *Daisy, Daisy, give me your answer, do!*, and boozy sentiment, *We all go the same way home*. And they asked her to sing them a 'foreign song', and so Anna, perched among them on firelight midnight, sang a song she recalled the soldiers singing as they came back from war, a sad low tune, translating the words as she traced them. 'Oh I would give my glory for my dear girl's heart, I'd plant my rifle for an apple tree.'

She saw tears stand in their eyes, and on her knees one of the scrawny cats purred.

They were human. She must love them or perish.

Later, another evening, they asked her for the song again, but after she had sung it, some of the footmen jeered.

"He was a proper simple one, wasn't he? Thinking the gun'd bloody grow into a sodding tree?"

Anna laughed too, as if they had just shown her the vast joke of existence. As they had.

On a special morning, Lilith Izzard came in to Hell.

"He's done with you then?" asked Mrs Ox.

"For now, he has." And Lilith cocked her fox eye at Anna. "Likes a change. I expect you were glad of the rest."

Anna shrugged. She was saying, "But you are the victrix." (Victrix, vixen.)

Lilith wore her servile dress, and was tying on her apron. Her hair hung long and loose from a white central parting.

Anna saw that Lilith had a Mediaeval face, as if from a painting, perhaps by the Dutch school. You might think the face was ugly, but studied, as you entered the time of its inception, you saw its fairness.

The face of Lilith was some centuries out of date. But she, truly, was a sorceress. So pale, her ginger hair so pale, her strange stranger's eyes.

"What are you staring at, Annie?" demanded Lilith. But there was no malice in her regard, not now.

Anna said, "He's an old bastard, that Raoul. But looks like he's done you good. You look that nice."

And the fox tossed her head.

"I'd give you a run."

"I bet you would, you horror. A bit of paint and you'd knock their eyes out." Anna made soft her own eyes. "Let me make up your face some night, Lily."

"And your dresses he bought you," said Lilith.

"Upstairs. If someone can bring them, you're welcome."

Lilith came over. She pinched Anna lightly on the arm.

"You're not so bad."

"No, I'm not so bad."

"But you're a bad girl, you are."

"So are you."

"It's men," said Lilith. She turned about to the whole room, flaunting at the footmen, the scullions, the boys. "They drag you down."

Greasy, gap-toothed, at the edges of all things, they jollied back at her. She had lifted them. They were Men. Magical and fearsome, mighty. Valid.

Anna thought, *No not so far off. That face...*

Lilith's face was, after all, from the sixteenth century. She resembled rather the young Elizabeth I, whose oak tree grew in the Basulte park.

And it was that evening Lilith took Anna up to the room of Raoul Basulte. For the male Basultes, apparently, were playing cards in the Smoking Room. They were drinking port and brandy, and would not be done till three or four in the morning. "And if he is," said Lilith, "if he finds us here, maybe he won't mind so much."

Anna had not been asked, or told, to wait on the Family. As many of the other servants did, she entered their apartments only when they were absent.

And now she saw Raoul's bedroom in the house, where she had never been.

How bizarre. Superimposed upon the hotels in Europe, the berths in trains, those cold little stops along the way.

There were two terrible stuffed masculine chairs before the black marble fireplace, and a table of newspapers, with a box of cigarettes, even a tobacco jar and some pipes like a gentleman's club.

The solid bed was draped in a kind of tartan rug of reds and browns, but above, the tester was crimson.

It smelled, the room, of male cologne, tobacco, and another faint smell, fusty, almost meaty, an odour Anna associated with adolescent young men, not very clean, living without some abrasive woman to chivvy them.

"See?" asked Lilith.

She drew Anna in and danced her about.

Anna waited for the curses and spittings to commence. But Lilith only pulled open the bed, and stood there smiling.

"Go on, you do it."

Anna went forward.

For a moment she felt inhibited and slightly sickened, which was her squeamishness, because of course what the servants did was perfectly right.

Then a rage swept through her. She spat violently into the centre of his smooth new sheet.

"Damn you, Raoul Basulte," she whispered. "I hope you rot in hell."

Lilith pranced, pleased. "Go on - go on..."

Anna took off her shoe. There was nothing in it, but she emptied it in the lower part of the bed below the sheet, secretively, as if there was.

"Fuck you, Raoul," said Anna.

Lilith crowed.

"He's a dirty dog," she cried.

But he was not a dog. They were the dogs. His bitches.

Lilith pushed her gently.

"Lie down. Go on. Let's lie in his dirty old bed."

Anna threw herself down and over, and lay on her back, her head on Raoul's pillows. Lilith leaned over her, then climbed lightly on her body.

They stretched there a few seconds, like folded

gloves in a box, the buttons of Lilith's dress pressing into Anna's breasts, as hers must do, she thought, into Lilith's.

Lilith's face, the flesh falling a little forward as she leaned up now and over Anna, swollen-looking and carnal, said, "I'll be him. I'll be Raoul."

And she began to jerk her hips forward and back, forward and back.

"Go on," said Lilith, to Anna, "tell him how grand he is."

So Anna called softly, "Oh Raoul, you're so lovely. Oh Raoul, how you fill me up!" Things she had never said, would never have thought to say, but which she knew Lilith would enjoy.

And Lilith shrieked thinly with mirth and jerked faster.

"It's not a fucking Derby, dearie," said Anna, remembering Lilian.

"Oh, I've got to, Annie, got to," whimpered Lilith, rolling her eyes. Had this happened? Did Raoul behave in this way, selfish and pathetic, when with his servant doxy?

"Oh wait, Raoul, please wait..."

"Oh I can't dear, no, no..."

"Oh Raoul..."

"Ooff! Ooff!" honked Lilith, grinding herself about on Anna's belly, bruising her perhaps. Lilith collapsed, and Anna patted her. "Did you love it, Lily?" whined Lilith, forgetting that Anna was only playing herself.

"Oh, yes, Raoul, you were wonderful. Like a stallion," said Anna. She found the awful witch's laugh rising in her, and let it crackle out of her lips and through the space under the tester.

"Do you love me, Lily?" Asked Lilith of herself.

"Oh, Raoul, I love you, I do, I do."

Insane merriment. They clung together, writhing in paroxysms of laughter in his bed. Anna was afraid neither of them would be able to stop.

Then Lilith pulled away and stood up, sober.

"We'd better tidy up."

And Anna's laughter too was utterly dismissed. They corrected the bed, pulled up the sheet and covers, folded them open again as in the best hotel. "When are you going to make me up?"

"When you like."

"Mousie brought your dresses down. Some weren't there. There were only two."

"You have them. "

"We'll put them on in our room."

Our room. And one dress for Anna, as well.

Lilith would have to be at work by four, or perhaps not. She would have concessions, surely. As Anna had.

They ascended the backstairs, up and up, and Lilith had brought a bottle of wine, stolen under the nose of Mrs Ox, she said, because long ago Lilith had acquired a copy of the butler's keys.

The butler wasn't one of them. The housekeeper was, for although Anna had never seen her in the kitchen, as she had only once seen the butler, Mrs Ox spoke of the housekeeper familiarly as Pinnie.

"When Pinnie was on the boards," had said Mrs Ox, only today, "she had a pair of legs that put them in a frenzy. Nothing else to her, mind. Jug of a face and no bosoms to speak of. But those legs kicked up a storm."

"Is it true," Anna had asked, since the cook had turned to her, expecting due reverence, "she was on the stage?"

"And she was a bad girl too," said Mrs Ox, "like you and Lilith."

Three bad girls.

The other girl from 'our room' had not come to bed. Lilith told Anna this girl, Mousie, slept more regularly with one of the footmen. She had been pregnant four times, and got rid of 'it' by drinking four cans of mustard in water. (*Another* bad girl.)

By the light of the soupy electric bulb, Anna saw two of her dresses spread like flat corpses on Lilith's narrow bed.

How tawdry they looked, after all. Had they always been of such poor quality?

One, greyish silk, the other black and stitched with lurid green beads.

"Redheads should favour green," announced Lilith, and took up this gown. "You dress me."

Anna said, subserviently naturally, "You'll have to take everything off, except your knickers."

"Naughty cow," said Lilith. "Got you excited have I?"

"You're better than Raoul," said Anna.

They laughed, shortly.

Lilith only stripped pragmatically and in fact totally. She was thin and wiry, with her little breasts set on like small soft-iced cakes, each with a cherry. But at her groin was the brush of the fox, redder than on her head.

Anna slid the beaded dress on to Lilith's body, and did it up.

"How do I look?"

"Undo you hair. "

Lilith unpinned the coil, and it fell down her, shining and slithering like a snake. Such long hair. It feathered her waist.

"A shame you can't wear it like that in the house."

"Just see old Madam's fat face if I did."

Anna recalled watching Lilith on a horse, dashed over the park behind Raoul, hair flying.

She put back the hair behind Lilith's left ear, and combed it out, flowering round the right side of her face. "We need a clip. And an earring."

But these had not been brought. Make-up had.

Anna sat Lilith on the bed.

Lilith had a touching innocent eagerness now, a reliance on Anna, quite frightening in such a frightening being, for she was really so chancy, Lilith, so potentially lethal. A demon that wanted to play, and let itself be tarted up. One wrong step, and she might bite or rend or invoke fire.

But no, Lily was a charming and wonderful girl. Anna was liking it so much, powdering her face this way, putting the mascara on her lashes, and a little on her pinkish eyebrows to darken them. And these scarlet lips.

Oh then. The last time she had made up another's face... at Preguna... just such ruby lipstick - oh, then.

"Why have you stopped?" challenged Lilith.

"I thought I heard a mouse."

"Probably did. Finish me. Come on."

Two or three more deft strokes. She had grown proficient, behind the dress shop at Preguna.

"There."

Lilith rose. She was imperious. She stalked to the mirror.

As Anna watched fondly, admiringly, Lilith fell head-over-heels in love with her reflection. She flirted with it, turning this way and that, once almost right round, looking back at herself over her own shoulder.

"*I'm* a pretty girl."

"Beautiful," said Anna. "I don't know about Pinnie. You're the one ought to be on stage."

"Oh, go on." This time it did not mean continue. Although, too, it did. And Anna took her cue.

"No, you're good enough for the films. You know, I've heard the producers just go round the city, in big cars, looking out for girls for a film. They want to find someone nobody's ever seen before. Some of the biggest names got started that way."

"The city? London, you mean?"

"Oh, yes. London, of course."

"I've never been to London." (Iner bin a lonun.)

"It would be fun to go," said Anna, "wouldn't it?"

Lilith spun to her with sparkling, black-lashed eyes. "What ud we do?"

Anna said, lazily, "Oh. Look in the big shops. Go to a cinema, watch a film. Eat in a fancy restaurant. Have a drink or two. Th'fellers ud be artor you, an no muztaikn."

"And the producer in his car?"

"He might. *Oh* yes. "

Lilith took up the wine bottle, filched from below and ready unsealed. She took a deep valorous swig. She passed the bottle to Anna. No matter the mouth of the bottle wasn't wiped. Anna had probably swallowed Lilith's saliva before, not to mention bathed in it.

"London," breathed Lilith. She added, "I was born in that pub. Jacko's Lizard. And then up here, scrubbing and running about. Once that old Raoul promised me we'd go."

"There are no trains, though," said Anna, vacantly.

"There's the car. Not that old rusty thing you came

back in. It's smart. Can go for miles."

"In the village? Whose car?"

"Me da's," said Lilith. She smiled radiantly and threw herself on to her bed, in the spangling dress and a flair of hair.

"Who'd drive?" Anna, wonderingly.

"I ud. He's taught me how."

Anna laughed. "When we goin?"

Powers of speech, of thought, realigning.

Lilith closed her eyes. "It's a dream. Sometime, never."

Emotion, like violent pain, lanced in Anna's body, between womb and brain. She knew she must not protest. She hadn't wanted to go, after all, escape, such things were not on her mind at all. Next second she heard Lilith begin, quietly, to snore. The exciting day had finally tired her out. Anna went and lay down on her own bed. She was trembling, weakly, her heart drumming against her ribs as if too strong for the rest of her.

Oh Christ, Christ. Would this monster remember? Tomorrow would she still desire London, the fairy tale producer, the glamours of an unknown country?

And did a proper car truly exist?

Anna turned on her side, away from Lilith Izzard.

It was useless to mourn. Ony binna bidda fun, hant it?

In the night somewhere, the dregs of it, before dawn began, Anna found Lilith lying close by her. Lilith caressed Anna's breasts. So Anna stroked Lilith's hair, and cradled Lilith's waist.

Eventually Lilith murmured, "Like a couple of those funny women, aren't we?"

"Are we?"

"Do you know what they do?"

"No," said Anna. (She lied.)

"No, they can't do anything," said Lilith mazily. "They haven't got anything, have they?"

"No."

"So if we tried," said Lilith, nuzzling into Anna's shoulder, "I expect it would be no good." ("Aspek ayud beena god.")

Anna lay still, her arms cramping, as Lilith resumed her snoring.

In the morning Lilith would wake her again, this time pinching her arm viciously.

Then Lilith would catch two flies from the wall to take down to Hell, for some breakfast dish of the Basultes'.

And Lilith said no more. She did not even come to the room with three beds, and was seldom in the kitchen.

They asked again for the foreign song. Anna sang it. They jeered and whistled, and guffawed and jested all through it. Anna laughed, so tickled by their acumen and wit, her bowels churning with an unnoted tumult.

Beyond the windows, the English rain fell, thick as slime.

It was evening, and they were preparing the dinner. They had not done very much to it, tonight. Perhaps they were enervated.

Mrs Ox turned from the ovens, ox-red. "Get up, you lazy minx. Get into the house and serve them. They want their drinks."

Anna was astonished. The ox-woman was talking

directly to her.

You mustn't argue.

"Yes, Mrs Ox."

She recalled the butler stationed in the salon, the maid and footman. She supposed she could serve drinks.

What was this? One of the girls was tying a new apron round her, and handing her, Oh God, the appalling Puritan bonnet.

Anna put the bonnet on. No one mocked her. Now they were pushing her out of the kitchen, and here was the stair, and then the footman was in front of her, opening the door into the Smoking Room.

"Don't fret. I'll tell you what to do."

The door was wide, and there was the room, and so the Basulte house, the part of it which belonged to the Family.

Anna was stunned, almost breathless. She was about to see them. To see Raoul, and Lilian and Tommy, and William. The Father, the Mother. These... gods.

They passed along a corridor. A maid trotted by, going elsewhere. Five days ago Anna had watched her sneezing in a pudding. She was different now.

Now they were going into the salon, its damp greenness, the blood-blotches of roses. The butler loomed at the sideboard, a bald ocean liner. All those bottles and glasses and none of it for them. Save what they stole.

They were lined up now, three correct dolls.

Anna felt a wave of vertigo. The Family was thrusting in, in a band again, a *tribe*. The Mother swept through first. She wore black, an awful gown with large black bows, and then came the Lilian-daughter, in a dress the colour of fresh gutted salmon, which was nauseous among the green, and would be unbelievable in the red dining-room.

The men followed. The too-young Father, with his greyed hair, and next the three younger males. But - they were so unalike, after all. Comparable only in the black hair and eyes. How stupid she had been to confuse them. And not handsome. Quite ugly. Particularly that one, who was, decidedly, Raoul.

Was she seeing them now as the servants always had, as servants always must? Hideous, and mindlessly obdurate in their power?

They had consigned her to this, because she would not be subservient and malleable in the first role they allowed her. She had let them down and tried to run away.

The footman nudged her sharply.

Anna recollected. For a moment she was resistant, and then she took a piercing lost delight in *bobbing* to the Basultes. She did it perfectly. She might have been trained, a cringing abasement faultlessly delivered. How simple it always was, to give in.

But as she hung her head before their might, Anna felt the breath on her neck of some mysterious and terrible fiend.

She only played a part, she acted to survive, and all the while, planned her second escape. Her father had loved such games and would have been peerless in this one. Yet she was not her father. And playing so well, taking pleasure in it all, a shadow was reaching for her out of some other dimension.

Oh, she must get free. For her time was running out. Could it be, her time as *Anna*, as her *self*?

The Basultes were talking. Their voices were a blur, and their educated English dialect as uncouth, and now nearly as indecipherable, as the vernacular of their slaves had been,

The footman kept whispering, helping her translate their wishes.

Drinks were manufactured. They seemed to make no sense at all, whisky with a spoonful apparently of hot sauce, and these ghastly green liquids, like squeezed alligators, which the women had ordered - what was in them? Only bottles were pointed out.

However, now she stood in front of Raoul, who she had met in a European city, when she was starving by its river. She offered up to him the tray with the very large whisky.

Anna the maid, her hair imprisoned under her cap, tied up tight in her starched apron.

"And how are you liking it, Ann?" She understood him. She stared, remembered, bobbed. And Raoul gave a ripe muscular laugh. "You learn quickly. Very nice, Ann. I'm proud of you."

"Thank you, sir," said Anna.

"We'll have you waiting in the Palace yet."

Lilian threw back her head and roared with amusement. Was it at his words? She had seemed to pay no attention.

And William was quarrelling with too-quick Derby Tommy by the fire, which tonight, despite the rain, was unkindled.

Anna kept her head dipped at the majesty of Raoul. She thought, *I spat on you.*

The shadow breathed on her neck. It was like a memory she had forced herself to forget, and had forgotten, and which now threatened to emerge and fill her skull with images of torn and bloody things. But it was not that. Memory she had never escaped.

"Thank you, Ann," said Raoul. Ah, she was to go. Dismissed. As she turned, he patted her bottom.

When the Family left the room, the butler also told Anna she might go. More experienced staff were required, it seemed, to attend the feeding of the gods.

All the stairs up to the attics were like a mountain. Anna climbed slowly, indifferently. She should return below. She would have to say she had felt ill. Which wouldn't do, would it?

When Anna woke, Lilith the Lizard's Daughter, was sitting on the foot of Anna's bed. Lilith wore her maid's black, but her hair was loose.

What now? A reprimand for retreating here and not going back to the kitchen.

"He says you're to come out, tonight."

"Who? Come where?" Anna had journeyed too far, asleep, to hope.

"In the park. Tonight."

"Why? Who?"

"Him. *Master*. That Raoul Basulte."

Anna lay bemused. The window was black, but pinned with a scatter of stars.

"Rain's stopped," said Lilith. "It'll be warm. The moon's up."

Anna sat. She smiled.

"You look lovely, even in that dress."

"Oh, I'm to be a film star, aren't I? When we two get to London."

"...That's just a dream, London."

Lilith winked. "Wait and see."

Anna lurched back. She shut her eyes and her heart drummed so loudly it broke the stars.

"He says, put on a dress. That grey one, maybe."

Who? Oh, Raoul, presumably. He wanted her out in the park in the grey dress, in the moonlight. But that was irrelevant. What was relevant were the words Lily had said. *Wait and see.*

Lilith was taking off her maid's uniform and pulling the beaded gown from under the bed, shaking it, putting in on.

"Come on, you," said Lilith, brisk and commanding. "Stur yer stumps."

Just like the poem, the white moon had climbed the summit of the sky. To the height it had had to go, the stairs of a tall house were nothing. And life was nothing. Fifty years, eighty years. The moon had done all of it, over and over.

Above the Basulte grounds, their park, (all muffled as if in black furs), the stars were big, and many had colours, yellow, sallow, or boiling white-blue.

It was a hot night, dry above and humid near the ground from the residue of rains.

Lilith bustled Anna along, up the avenue of chestnuts and aside, through a landscape which now seemed quite intemperate under the oaks and ranging cedars.

"Are there foxes?"

"Oh yes, Annie. And badgers too. And sometimes they fight."

Anna shuddered. Badgers were a sort of bear, weren't they? Did wolves still run in the English forests? In fact she wasn't certain. She was so ignorant. Always, probably, would be.

They came into a sort of grove, and some of the maids were there, not clothed as maids now, but in cheap party dresses, awful frilled, badly-draped things, stitched up by mothers or one-eyed village dress-makers.

One of the boys stood under a tree. He was tuning up a violin. Would he play badly? Why play at all?

Then, through the trees, a groom came, guiding a coal-black horse.

For a second, the whole scene, blaringly-lit by the high moon and sulphurish stars, had the grotesqueness of a Goya sabbat: the girls with loose hair and bare arms, the boy fiddler against the great hewn shape of the tree, and this nightmare horse, black as some devil animal in a story, shaking its head, stepping over the roots and through the weeds, the drifts of strange wild English flowers.

"Who'll ride him?" called the groom across the glade "Is it you, Lily Izzard?"

"No," said Lilith in a hard cool voice. "It's her. He wants *her* on it."

"Oh, no," said Anna. "I can't ride."

"No matter," said Lilith.

Anna was light, humorous. "But I'll fall off."

"Better not to," said Lilith, hard now as a slim cold stone.

The groom strode over. Ho was a rough man she had seen before, in the kitchen, slurping his sugary black tea from a saucer.

"Up you go."

"My dress," said Anna, reasonably.

The groom stood looking at her, at her lower body, where the gown clung over her hips and thighs.

"You see to it, Lily," said the groom.

And Lilith moved around Anna. She leant down, and taking two handfuls of the silk skirt, ripped them apart.

Anna felt a primeval awe, as if her skin instead had been torn wide as a curtain.

The gown only just covered her, now, parting about an inch below her crotch. She put, her hand there, involuntarily, and realized she must look like a coy Venus on a shell.

The groom was lifting her anyway. There was no chance to protest or resist. She was there already, on the horse's back, sitting awkwardly side-saddle. "Swing thee lug oover." said the groom impatiently. He looked up now, waiting for the flash of her most private part. But she pulled the skirt upward to cover herself as she eased her right leg to the other side of the horse.

Now she sat bareback on it. It was restive, and she felt the rolling muscles in its top, and smelled its hot wet smell. How could she have imagined this might be erotic? She was afraid, and clutched the horse's mane. She had no idea what to do with the horse.

On the ground - far down - the servants in the grove were voraciously laughing at her, their little cruel eyes very bright. Anna laughed too, to show them how clever they were and how she approved of everything they did.

But her body was shaking with alarm. The horse jerked and ambled, free of the touch of the groom, and sensing doubtless only panic from Anna, her knees gripping, slipping, her hands pulling at its mane and trying to find, hopelessly, purchase on its neck. She called out, blithely. "What do I do?"

"You're all right. He won't bolt. Maybe."

But they would tire of this jest in a few minutes. She had noticed before, such people often lost interest swiftly in all things, even their dearest and most perverse pursuits.

131

She patted the horse's neck firmly. "Steady," she said.

The horse shied its head from her. Damnable thing. It hated her too.

The fiddler had struck up a tune abruptly. It was syncopated, and modern, some song that might be heard on a gramophone record.

The horse began to walk through the grove. Frozen, Anna sat rigidly upright. The horse took her slowly, decidedly, practiced, across the lines of girls and men, and into the thick trees beyond.

At once, the moon melted into darkness. The horse stepped on. Behind them, the laughter and jibes merged away like the light.

Nerves tingled in Anna's spine. They were deep into the nightness of the park. Fragrance rose from the flowers and clover beaten by the rain, crushed now by the hooves of the horse.

She wanted to call, but there was no one to call to. There had never been, of course.

Anna sat still, facing through the dim ghost-greyness that filmed between the tree trunks.

A firefly sparkled. It was a cigarette. Raoul walked out into her path.

"Where are you going?" he asked. Like a prince meeting a royal fairy-lady in the wood.

Bleakly Anna ordered her mind. But she was suddenly sick of it now. So bloody sick of them all. She had tried so hard. These games. Always these foolish deadly games.

"I don't know," she said, "Raoul."

"Well, I think you came to find me, didn't you, Ann?"

"Oh, yes," she concurred listlessly. Tears pushed inside her eyes. She held them in, and instead her eyes began to burn and ache.

Raoul now was guiding the horse.

Distantly, she heard a couple of loud communal cries back in the grove. The fiddle sawed and squeaked. But here in the dark was another world.

"You're a treasure. Ann," he said. "You're worth a lot to me."

"Am I?"

"Yes, Ann. I like you like that, all dolled up. I liked you in the apron, too. Your quaint little curtsy. You're awfully good, Ann. I knew you would be."

"Thank you."

He must have indicated something to the horse. It stopped. Raoul came around its body, and put his hands on her bared leg.

She said, "The dress got torn."

"I'll buy you another."

"When we go to London?" she asked, before she could control her tongue.

Raoul laughed softly. He ran his hands up her leg, and clasped the join of her body, and a thrill of disgusting arousal stabbed through her, but divorced from her utterly, as though mind and flesh had separated.

"Shall I mount?"

She said nothing. He swung up on to the horse as if it were no trouble at all. He was behind her. And for him, the horse kept still.

Raoul slipped his arms around her. He fondled her breasts, pressing into her body.

"Do you like this?"

"Yes."

"It's better when he gallops. Like to try it?"

"No," she said, "I'll fall..."

"I'll keep hold of you." he said. And he kicked the horse in the side.

Anna screamed.

"Yes," said Raoul.

The trees miraculously parted. They were flying over rough tumbling open ground, and the moon raced with them overhead.

Every leap of the muscles of the horse slapped Anna upward, and as her body came down each time his fingers penetrated her more deeply.

She was sick with fear and lust. Her head flung itself back. She thought in a moment she would be dead, but she wouldn't feel it.

Only what he did to her, this ugly grunting man, mattered.

She had let go of the horse. The monster, Raoul, kept her on, kept her from being dashed away. Omnipotent.

When it ended, she was crying. Raoul sat behind her, swigging from a silver flask, He did not offer it.

"Wonderful Ann," he said. "Remember, I won't let you go. You belong to us. You know I'd kill you, if you ran away again. And; anyway, where would you go? To hell and back, eh? But you understand. It's sorted out now, isn't it? You just needed a bit of guidance. Eh?"

"Yes," she said.

They rode back. He controlled the horse expertly, a bit of guidance. Anna seemed boneless, mindless. She had lost everything, surely. Or, only realised that she had lost everything already, long ago.

In the grove, men and women fornicated in couples and in heaps. With his shirt off, the fiddler played. Some danced.

Raoul got off the horse, then pulled Anna quickly and easily down and passed her immediately over into another man's arms, like a dancer.

Was this William? Or Tommy...

"She's all warm."

"She's warm enough."

She was on her back, (the wet bath of the grass), and the man was astride her. "Struggle a bit," he invited her.

Like a puppet worked by God, Anna struggled a bit, and he slapped her face quite softly, and climaxed.

There were two or three more. Perhaps the same ones more than once. None of them hurt her, not even the slap had done much more than sting. It was no worse than had happened here and there, before.

In the end, there were no men, and Lily flopped down beside her. She had brought a bottle of lemonade spiky with gin. Tired children at a picnic.

"What a night," said Lilith, satisfied.

They lay, looking up at the stars, their bodies half bared, splashed by the lusts of their masters, their own.

"Thought I'd forgotten, hadn't, you," said Lilith, as if this were only an ordinary evening, and some mundane place. Nearby rose gigglings and a rusty rhythmic and prolonged shrieking of female orgasm.

"Forgotten," said Anna.

"Got that car," said Lilith. "Run off shall uz?"

Anna shut her eyes. Raoul would not let her run. Raoul had taken command of her. She had allowed it. The world was the horse, and death up behind her, making love. (The stars were dirty, and seemed to be going out.)

"Lonun," said Lilith throatily. "Bet as you know sumon can make me a star."

Chapter Eight: A Nocturne; with Extended Coda

Such hot nights, that late summer, at Preguna. The open windows brought no air, only traffic sounds, and moths. But the pot of dorisa redly bloomed on and on, like an unquenchable fire.

How long had she been with him? A month, or less. The time seemed longer. Shorter.

But now she would wake up sometimes, from the heat, about three or four in the morning, before the first ephemeral cool of the predawn.

Anna would pace quietly about the room, which now also was hers, *theirs*. She was careful not to wake him.

Sometimes she sat in the basket-work chair, and watched him sleep. He was silent and almost entirely still. Very occasionally, he would turn on his side or back, and once he spoke distinctly to someone in a dream. She leaned close to hear if it were herself, yet couldn't be sure.

The light was warmly silvery, and everything, except for Árpád, insubstantial. She often thought, watching him, how handsome he was, and the mark on his face so beautiful, like the colour painted on the wing of a butterfly, or across some exotic leaf.

Asleep, he hid nothing. He was lean as a white lion, naked, the sheet spilled.

At last she would lie down beside him. In the brief coolness, it was reasonable to touch, and draw near.

Now and then he woke. They amalgamated in a

dislocated and surrealistic way. She did not like to press for this, because she sensed a weakness in him, a tiredness. Yet at other times of day or night he would take her now, swiftly and surely, his urgent love-making halting stammeringly only in order not to be too quick for her.

Best, he liked the dark of night - of course - their bodies and faces gliding pane on pane, invisible, only tactile.

It was one early morning, however, the light only just beginning to remember it might exist, when she began to search among his things.

She knew this was wrong. She sensed in herself some impulse, but had no idea what it was. She was curious, insatiable, eating up everything about him. And his privacy should not be attempted.

So, she did not read the letters she found in bundles under his folded garments in a drawer, nor did she pick the lock, (she could pick locks, sometimes), of the cash box he kept. Old correspondence, money - what were these?

In the end, though, behind the books stacked two or three deep in the frontless cabinet, she found a small bottle, stoppered shut and sealed, like a fine old wine.

She knew. Must have known - her search. She held the bottle to the waking window, but it was only black. How cold it felt to her.

When she had replaced it, she lay down on the bed far off from him, nervous he would feel culpability on her skin.

He was to go and see to his accountancy somewhere, and their breakfast was hurried. When he returned, it was dusk.

Anna had laid the table and put purple flowers in a bowl, left wine to cool in the basin.

They drank a little of the wine.

"I took a book from the cabinet," she said artlessly, "and a funny little bottle fell out. It looked such an odd little bottle."

Árpád glanced at her. Frequently he forgot to shield his face from her, but abruptly he turned now, shielding it. Against the blue-gold of the window, his profile, the left side, was chiselled and expressionless.

"Oh. Really. Did you try to open it?"

"No. Is it yours?"

"Yes, Anna."

Anna said, "What could it be?"

"Have you heard of Pandora?"

Anna shuffled papers of memory. "She undid a bottle?"

"In a way. All the ills of the world got out. But the last thing to escape was hope."

She went to a side table, where she had set some food. She began to slice tiny pieces of vegetables even smaller.

"Don't worry about it, Anna."

"Of course I will."

"It was a long time ago that I got it. Years ago. In case I found, in the end - I couldn't go on with it."

"Yes."

"It's painless. The chemist promised me. He - showed me. The little mouse, it simply curled up quite happily in its straw, and went to sleep for ever. One need only take a small spoonful. But, I wanted to be sure."

She cut the loaf, and seemed to stand thirty feet in the air, working the sharp knife in the cooked dough by a process of directive magic having nothing to do with sight or hands.

"Please just forget you found it, Anna."

A torrent rushed against her brain. She wanted to fling herself at him, crying that it must be thrown away, he must never, *never...*

Her mouth was wise, refusing to form these words.

She said nothing, and then, when Árpád said again, uncertainly, "Anna?", Anna said, "Of course. I'm sorry. Let's talk about something else."

That night they went walking through Preguna, among the shadows. There were posters up under the lamps, reminding the city of approaching carnival.

In the bed, they made love. As he came against her, slipped aside, kissed her, slept, she thought of the mouse, going to sleep so peacefully in its straw.

She waited several days, and nights. She wasn't sure that he would trust her; perhaps he would. But probably, most likely, he would check the bottle had been replaced, and left alone.

When she thought there had been enough time, one day when he was gone, she took the poison bottle out again.

She couldn't quite bring herself to destroy it. It was, if horribly, his property, and in any case, poured down a drain or thrown away outside, might kill other blameless things, beasts, or children. She hid it as best she could.

Anna had known about the carnival at Preguna since she had first been there. People had talked to her, reminisced about it. Even the old professor.

He had, apparently, masked himself as a ram, and danced in a ballroom with a woman of mystery and charm. She had not been masked, simply had had her face painted, partly black and partly silver, and somehow this had made it useless for him to try to guess who she might be, and she had known that too, flirting and leading him on. She was not truly, (naturally), the sort of woman he preferred. But carnival galvanised and disorientated. For three days and nights after, he had been haunted by her presence, the memory of her voice.

Peepy too, at the shop, had held the girls spellbound, (blondes, brunette, redhead, sitting naked, smoking), with the tale of how a young man had pursued a young woman all through the carnival, he in his immaculate dinner clothes, and she in a starry gown, only her eyes concealed by a wisp of tinsel. He had possessed her at last in a stationary carriage among some nightingaled gardens. But as the dawn flowed in, the fatal woman dissolved in scented powder. She was only some exquisite ghost, cursed for ever to lure men to her on that single lawless night.

Anna had said to Árpád, they might go out, mightn't they? For she was also lured by the stirring excitement, the prickling and elasticity of the air, as if before a storm.

He had, she knew, a set of perfect evening garments, night-black, moon-white, left from some unavoidable function. And she had the moon-white dress he had bought for her, after she had run to him in it.

She bought a slender mask, a white moth, with diamond-sequinned eye-holes. She described herself to him in this garb; her lips lipsticked crimson, her opalescent hair sleeked in the diamanté clip.

"All right, Anna. If you want. I know, it's a fever, the carnival. I've watched from the window..."

Anna thought of photographs seen of the carnival, the masks, or faces spectacularly painted, a man speckled like a leopard, a woman whose cheeks were transformed to flowers like some glorious leprosy.

Árpád was reluctant. What else? No, no, he was terrified. She could not give him quarter.

And carnival arrived.

Long before the sun had gone, revellers were on the streets. The trams clanked up and down, and other vehicles hooted, and the gold leaf of the falling sun showed her, leaning from the window, the garlanded figures, the black and white men, the women who were rainbows, the children running, and none, none of them with a properly human face. A night of animals, phantoms, and secrets, walking on two legs.

She had bathed and used perfume. She dressed in the white dress, and did her hair. At the mirror he had bought for her, Anna made up her face, darkening her lashes, affirming her lips. She put on her mask, and a moth enclosed her eyes. She felt utterly suddenly, like a hundred thousand others, *I am no longer myself. I am in disguise. Now I may do as I wish.*

At this instant, Árpád appeared behind her in the mirror.

"Anna - how wonderful you look." His voice was hollow and too low.

"Hurry and dress," she said. "Where is your mask?"

"Anna - Anna forgive me. I've been - dreading this. No, Anna. I won't."

She did not turn to him, but drew her head up, eyes masked, set free. In the mirror she confronted him.

"You're handsome, Árpád. You don't see it."

"Anna, don't be a fool."

141

"Beautiful. Like a prince. You..."

"Be quiet, Anna," harshly now. "Don't insult me."

His face, turned sidelong, speaking from the edge of itself. Not looking at his own disfiguration.

She raised the lipstick in her hand, and whirled it over the mirror glass, a long bloody strand.

"You don't have any care for me," she said arrogantly.

He turned from her almost entirely.

"You don't trust me," she said. "You think I've lied to you."

"I think - oh God, Anna, I think you see me in a way no one else can. I *cherish* you for that. But the rest..."

Moving, his face, its clear left side, all in the coalescence of the light, reflected behind the streak of lipstick on the mirror.

Anna stood alone in stasis.

Presently, after a minute, she could speak. "Árpád..." and then in a rush, "let me do something. Let me try."

He was tired. In despair, he had put on the splendid evening clothes. They must have weighed like lead. His shoulders sagged.

"What?"

"Sit down. Sit there, where the light falls."

"Why?"

"Please, please - just for a moment. If you trust me at all."

He sat in the chair and shut his eyes.

Anna came to him, predatory, in the aura of sunfall and some ancient holy madness.

"What - what are you doing?"

"It's nothing. Keep quite still."

She had stroked the lipstick, carnelian red, upon the

carnelian birthmark, and so drew the colour sidelong. She had bridged his nose, and ended in a curlicue, a scarlet feather, under his left eye. As God had done, she painted him. The colour of the butterfly, the hot-house leaf, the serpent, the Bird of Paradise. She drew a second tendril upward, over his chin, the second feather. And down from the mark that branded his forehead, she brought the third feather, to the hollow of his left cheek.

And now, now Árpád was merely a god, of fire and blood. Marked for the warrior jewel, but only painted, as if before the battle of life.

"Open your eyes." She was standing in fear and joy before what she had done, the completion of the act, translated by her human hand so as to be understood.

And his eyes did open, so blue, so wide, and she was in the presence of a divine and terrible being.

"What have you done?" he said, not angrily, bemused, feeling the power she had unleashed, the room thrumming full of it, and he its centre.

"Look in the glass."

He blinked, and then got up and went to the mirror.

She could not see his face, he stood only straight and completely immobile.

Anna was frightened. Afraid he would now deny this, smear it away. Which would be sacrilege.

He stood on and on. And she did not dare to go closer, to see what he saw.

And then he said, flatly, "It looks as if it's only paint. All of it. Just paint for the carnival." And then he said, "Do I look like that?" And she knew he also had seen himself at last, and for the very first time.

Preguna at night - oh, did she only imagine it? - was

supernatural. Gilded by lamps, with gold leaf on the buildings, and the moon so bright.

It was like - afterwards she sought for analogies - those places said to exist beyond death, another country more beautiful, and completely amiable, representing the landscapes and cities of the world, yet perfect. Heavenly. Where you might experience the raptures that had been denied to you on earth.

The air smelled sweet, of flowers and perfumes, and tindery from the fireworks that in bursts were let off in the parks.

There were crowds, but all moving so easily and fluidly, as if scheduled by master choreographers. There was no roughness. The sudden inadvertent touches were like those of happy children, and yet shy and gentle as deer.

Where did they go? It had become mixed in her mind. Tram rides, and rides on wagons drawn by horses garlanded in flowers and ribbons, walking the long streets, and dancing in the cathedral square, where orchestra succeeded orchestra. And there were Mediaeval peasant dances, partners parting, running away, swirling back again, and kisses exchanged. And there were waltzes, rather bumpy on the uneven ground, and preposterous flouncing tangos.

Árpád knew them all. She did not ask him how. Somehow she deduced that he had learned them in secret from books, practicing with a shadow in his arms, in that room now theirs.

At first, he had kept on turning his head at its angle, once or twice even feeling after his hat, as if it might have blown off. But then he would catch sight of himself so often, in the reflective surfaces of windows, brass plaques set on walls, and other faces; all the mirrors of the night.

They had not gone as far as the first lighted café, when seven or eight young girls, vaporous in gauzes, and in little eye-masks like Anna's own, skeined past, and, brazen with carnival, pointed at Árpád, laughing and exclaiming, and one even called to him in another language of the far south, saying how handsome he was.

Árpád and Anna both grasped this language sufficiently to understand her words.

He had been turning his head aslant for the first, and now his head snapped up. Later, as he relapsed and revived, faltered, altered, he was finally straightened out like a man cured of paralysis. Not only the way he held his neck and face had changed. His slim hard body was upright now. He moved with power. So that by the time they danced, his whole persona was his true self.

Soon they were also slightly drunk. There was so much to drink, wine and spirits, and liqueurs, the offered bottles of strangers in the heavenly city, where all were one, and there could be no harm, the drinking parties by the cafés, where anyone might pause.

Anna rang with happiness like a bell, or a champagne glass. Light flowed right through her. Her eyes were crystals. She stepped in winged slippers. And he was gold.

His marvellous thick soft fair hair, with its white blondness on the right side, was now like spectacular plumage. And the colours of his face, his blazon.

He was proud after all, and incredibly strong. He lifted her in the air as they danced, laughing up at her face, which now, briefly, was higher than his own.

Girls everywhere fluttered when they saw him. In the square, right through the crowd of dancers, came one splendid woman, with the impossible loveliness of a film actress, a face formed of white porcelain, obscured only where the mask around her eyes made her an owl with outstretched wings. And she handed Árpád a rose.

She was tall. Her dress was black satin, and on her wrist was a bracelet of emeralds. Ignoring Anna, this chimaera looked deeply into his eyes. She murmured, "I would die for you." And drawing herself up, kissed his lips. This done, she swept away.

Anna was not discomposed. In her bubble of silver glass, she needed to fear no other sorceress. Besides, Árpád turned back to her at once. "If she wants to kiss so boldly, she shouldn't eat so much garlic."

Anna saw he was a purist, a prude. She had always, perhaps, known it. Then, exactly then, it didn't matter. Yet, she was for an instant half offended. The woman had been so beautiful. Garlic on her breath was an irrelevance, unless you hated garlic, which Árpád did not. Criticism did not belong to this night.

And Anna shrugged. "What a stern judge."

"You've ruined me," he said. "Always so fresh and fragrant."

But these things a man could say who had never been afraid. *You've ruined me for other women* - The choice.

Her happiness ringed her. She had given him this and shown him - shown him - but what had she shown him? Ah, shown what was his own true worth.

Now he saw that he was stared at for his exceptional qualities, stared at in admiration and envy. He had taken to it so quickly, too, as if, like the dances, he had practiced for this hour. Perhaps he had done so in dreams.

Sometimes, even dancing with him, she saw him objectively. On this night of rarities and display, when everyone was set free, of them all he was the most splendid, his escape Promethean.

They ate supper at one of the hundreds of tables, near the lake, over which the fireworks arced and rained, platinum and diamond and gold.

One wine bottle was empty, so they ordered another.

The light splashed on them. On the upturned flowers of so many faces.

He no longer turned his head aslant. Fire burned on his skin. His eyes were wide, as if to devour the sky and every light of Preguna. He *bathed* in the sun of the light.

It was simple to enter the palace of delight, this memory of great happiness, liberation and reward. But from the palace there was only one gaping exit, a descent to tumult and despair.

She had never been able, afterwards, to relive the joy of the carnival. Because, following through shining room after shining room, she must come to the last doorway and the roaring descent.

However, just as Árpád must sometimes have dreamed he walked the city arrogantly in daylight, his face like that of any other attractive man, so now and then in dreams Anna could be returned into heaven.

In the dreams, heaven did not always finish in the same way. Very often she was able to wake up before the full gamut had been run.

Even if she did dream of the night's ending, she had never dreamed it quite as it had been.

Her brain wouldn't permit her, perhaps, to suffer that more than once.

By tradition, the carnival ended with the sounding of the three o'clock bell from the cathedral.

Tanith Lee

Then a silence fell on the revellers. Then there started a handful of outbursts of rebellious noise. Then again, silence. Like all creatures of the night, they must slink away before the dawn began.

Here and there, a last slow dance was played by an exhausted band, some unmasked and kissed, exchanging mementoes and promises.

Yet everywhere they rose, the celebrants, from their gilded Mass, in floating islands of dismissal. And like the sparks of the dying fireworks, humanity went drifting away, dissolving down the darkness into the reality of another world less real than heaven-on-earth.

Árpád and Anna walked slowly, as so many couples did, worn out, tipsy, soft with premonitions of sleep.

She did not think. Had not thought it out. It wasn't so much that the theatre of the night had convinced her, *fooled* her. For it had revealed only what she had always known.

"I'm so tired. Thank God you don't have to get up. We can sleep till noon."

"Yes," he said.

Already his voice was distant. But only, in the way of a voice which was tired.

"What a lovely night it's been."

"Yes."

"Darling," she said.

They had been holding hands. Now his hand dropped hers. She recalled how he had put the unwanted rose the woman gave him, into his water glass on the table. That had been more tender than this.

Almost, she began to ask him what the matter was.

Later, she could scarcely believe her stupidity.

Had her stupidity, even, been wicked? As if she had

148

let go her baby out of a window through carelessness, simply because she was looking at a bird in the sky.

She knew. Everything at once. She said, nevertheless, very carefully, as if testing the words in case they were too hot, "You must be so tired."

"Yes."

"I'll make some chocolate when we get in. The Italian chocolate you like. Shall I?"

"If you want."

"Mm," she said, in a quiet cheerful little voice, and chunks of terror surfaced in her bloodstream and around her heart, beginning slowly to asphyxiate her.

They walked on.

A tram rumbled by, its windows unlit. It was like a lumbering hearse on wires.

The remaining figures in the streets resembled ghosts. And yet she wanted to run to them and beg them for their help. They would do nothing. They had already done enough.

When they reached the apartment house, he went up the stairs ahead of her. He left her to come after him, or perhaps to go away.

What she did was silly and pitiable. She dawdled on the stair, pretending she had some trouble with her shoe, as if everything were ordinary. As if nothing had happened. Or ceased to happen.

When she reached his floor, the door of the room stood ajar. There was just space for her to squeeze inside. This gave her a moment's hope. She had thought, she realized now, that he would close the door - not lock it, but shut it tight. As if she didn't belong there at all.

But when she entered the room, which had been his, and next theirs, no lights were lit, only the faint upflung glow of the street came in, and the dimmest pearl, not white or grey, was beginning on the sky.

In the semi-dark, Árpád knelt at the book cabinet, and she saw he had pulled out the books already and put them, quite neatly, on the floor.

Anna shut the door at her back. For they were naked now.

"Where is it?" he said, not loudly.

"What, darling?"

"You know what, Anna. Where?"

"No, I don't kn..."

He got up and turned to her. His eyes were two bulbs of nothingness. He said, louder now, "*Where?*"

"I haven't..."

"Yes, Anna, you have. You took the bottle out. What did you do with it?"

She put back her head. She challenged him angrily, "Why do you want it?"

"Why do you think?"

"Then you mustn't have it, must you?"

He took a stride towards her. He was fierce, like the whirlwind, and she was afraid of him, but only for a second.

He had stopped himself. He looked at her, and she could see him again inside his eyes. Some of him, at least.

"Dearest Anna, you only mean to be good, I know. But you really must let me have it."

A dim returning anger made her say, "Why are you so selfish, Árpád? What about me?"

"You..." His body was bowing over a little again, as it had always done. A slight stoop, what you might expect of a young man who worked at the accounts of others.

Then he put up his hands and smeared his face

quickly over. The red salve bloodied and washed about, and out of it the true red reappeared, the warrior brand of the birthmark. "Look at me," he said. And then, "Anna, I've had tonight. You gave me that. You meant only the best for me. Can't you see what you've done?"

Anna trembled. Head up, she faced him, as if in the dock judges in black accused and condemned her.

"There's only one night of carnival, Anna."

"Well, then..." she faltered. She said rashly, "We just have to go back to what we had before. It was all right. It's what you've always done."

"Till now," he said.

"But you saw..."

He said, "All my life, since I was aware, I've *seen*. How they look at me, or won't look. When I was a child. When I tried to learn to be a priest and love a God who did this to me, and make myself beloved in turn so no one would *mind* my face... And tonight, I lived as the gods live, Anna. The real gods. That bitch with her rose and her stinking breath - and the pretty girls blushing - and you in my arms..."

"I love you," she said. "I did it because I love you. Please - let's just lie down and sleep. You're so strung up, how can you be reasonable...?"

"How can I be reasonable, yes, Anna. How can I? Can't you understand? I can't go back to what I was. A year of that, waiting for carnival night again? No, not even with you, Anna. You were everything, but you're not enough, not now. I want to be a human man. Only that. Not even this handsome prince you make believe I am. Just nothing, someone who can come and go unnoticed. Like the rest of you."

She clasped her hands across her waist. She seemed

to stand on a narrow plank above a twisting sea that had no floor.

"Árpád - forgive me - I only wanted..."

"I forgive you, Anna. I know. Don't distress yourself. Now tell me where the bottle is."

She lowered her head. She closed her eyes. Behind the mask she still had on, behind her shut lids, he could not see her.

"No."

She had expected his rage probably, almost anything, but not what happened.

He was so gentle with her, even in the act of sex. Sometimes when moths came into the apartment, he had caught them in a goblet and set them free into the night.

When he struck her, reeling, almost falling, she thought it was some other thing, an accident of weather or some part of the ceiling crashing down.

But he struck her again, and she lay on the floor, tasting a thin trickle of blood from her lip.

She stared up at him. And he stood above her, enormous in the sombre hollow of the room, waiting.

"Tell me," he said, breathless and hoarse, and catching her hands he pulled her halfway up and slapped her face again.

Had she cried out? She thought not. It had been so immediate, her screams, unuttered, were left behind.

As he dropped her back her head banged on the floor. She thought idiotically, *I have to tell him.* But she couldn't remember what she was to tell. And when he ordered her again to tell him, she shook her stunned head, more in confusion than denial.

Then he kicked her. The blow was awful. Alive on its own, it didn't hurt, yet threw everything else away.

The blow was so far removed from him. He was no longer Árpád, but some madman who had broken in.

She rolled sideways, and curled herself up by the table, which still bore a scatter of their normal life, plates, glasses, for these objects clattered, jittered, as he moved about the room.

He tore things apart in the room. Her few clothes, one curtain. Oddly he did not go to her bag lying in the bottom of the cupboard.

It was violence he wanted most, and acquiescence. She must give him the poison, drag it and present it to him on her knees. Tonight she was the one to blame. But she must answer now for all the world, which had hated and harried him and driven him insane.

Dully she thought, *He'll kill me anyway.*

And in that moment he turned and veered back towards her, blundering mechanical and blind, like the darkened tram.

The light must be coming, morning, or a fire. There was redness on the room, and he was in the eye of it, the storm of the redness.

His face was unrecognisable, rags of scarlet and grey. His eyes were framed in blood.

Now she did wail in a fey lost voice, *No, no,* something like that, as he pulled her up once more.

He did not demand anything of her. He shook her, and she thought her skull would crack from her neck, but then she was falling and again the table rattled, and round her dropped, fellow casualties, bits of china, glass, cutlery, and the pot of dorisa, also red, to break and shatter. He trod the glass and blooms under, and drawing back his foot, he kicked her again, full in the stomach.

This was death. Surely it was. Blackness bulged, with

inflamed edges, nausea, and a swimming out. Voices called in ocean.

Then only one voice, Árpád's voice, shouting in her face, his spittle hitting her like the foam.

She felt it under her hand, and brought it round, not really thinking, and slid her arm powerlessly, half-caressingly, up his body, as if making love to him. And then she stroked over his shoulder and stuck the knife, the sharp knife from the bread, straight into his throat, where she knew, even in the state she had reached, that it would kill him.

There was no longer noise, but for a throbbing and grinding in her ears. Hot sea water had dashed her face and neck, nothing else, and then one last heavy light thing, his arm falling across her body, as it had sometimes done in deepest sleep.

When she woke, the day was already beginning to be hot. Light flushed the room.

She had been sleeping by him on the floor, and he was still asleep. How silly of them, not to have moved to the bed. But it had been the night of carnival, hadn't it?

Anna knew she had drunk too much. Her head, her entire face and body, ached, and in her belly there was a large black stone, heavy, and pulling on her. She got up, and retched, but then the illness subsided. She drank some water. She took her bag from the cupboard. What an odd way that curtain hung...

She would have to go quickly to the shop. She was very late, she knew she was.

Only as she went down the stairs did she think she had not said goodbye to him, or even tried to wake him. But then, he would want to sleep.

On the street, people glanced at her, very often. She must look a sight. She had forgotten to wash her face and comb her hair.

And she had the dress on still, the white dress. And look, she had spilt some red wine on it, like the other girl with the expensive jacket.

But she owned this dress. Árpád had bought it for her. The stain didn't matter.

On the tram, it came to her she still had on her mask, which covered the eyes. She thought of taking it off, but simply couldn't be bothered.

On the tram too she was stared at, but then they turned away. Once an old woman came up to her. The old woman spoke to her in a hushed voice, and Anna could not understand what she said. All at once, she had forgotten the language of this place. How strange, she had been in the city for a year or more - or was she mistaken? What was the name of this place?

As she was getting off the tram, somehow she fell to her knees.

Some people rushed up to her and tried to lift her, questioning her anxiously, excitedly.

Anna grasped some of the words. She said, but only in French, "No, thank you. I'm quite all right. Please don't distress yourself." She said this brightly and firmly, to show she knew her own mind. She was acutely embarrassed.

Someone else had said to her, she thought, that about not distressing herself. But Anna wasn't distressed.

She walked trimly along the street to the dress-shop, and went straight through, where an assistant stood, her hands flying up to her mouth like hungry birds.

There was no one in any of the back rooms, nor in the

dressing room. Some flies buzzed in tangerine sunlight. Even empty, there was the smell of scent and make-up and women.

It was a nice smell, Anna had liked it. Now she doubled over, and water erupted from her throat and mouth.

When she raised her head, the lesbian woman, Peepy, was poised in the doorway in her dark blue muslin.

Anna laughed, still embarrassed.

"I'm so sorry. I drank too much last night. How awful. And I'm late."

Peepy said slowly, as if she too were finding her way about in an alien language, "No, it's only morning yet, Anna. Why don't you sit down?"

And then Peepy came up to her and led her to the chair, and sat her there.

"Oh, my dear," said Peepy.

Anna thought, after all, Peepy was going to want to make love to her. And although Anna didn't mind, she hoped Peepy wouldn't, exactly now. For Anna felt so sick, so dizzy, and this stone in her womb weighed so heavily and hurt so much, and there was another pain too, but what was it?

Peepy had put a second chair in front of Anna, and raised her legs gently on to it. Then she pulled Anna's skirt right up to her hips. Oh God.

"It's all right, darling," said Peepy, "don't be frightened."

"No, I'm not - but - couldn't we wait a little."

"No, darling. We mustn't wait."

But what was Peepy doing? She had bundled a costly garment, now another, from the rail, and was stuffing them in quite hard up between Anna's legs.

Anna giggled with genuine astonished laughter.

"What *are* you doing, Peepy dear?"

"Nothing at all, darling. Just sit quite still. See if you can't have a little sleep. I'll be back in only a moment."

And as Anna sank away, downwards, somewhere, glad to have been given permission, she saw Peepy amusingly run out of the room, and far off heard her frenziedly shouting, incomprehensible words, as if war had come and an invasion.

Margot, (her name) had a rambling apartment in an affluent area of Preguna, which she shared with the elderly, eccentric and kohl-eyed female lover who had shouted *Harlot* at the dress-show. This woman, Peepy - Margot - introduced to Anna, not by name, but, by a title. "This is my Great Love."

And the Great Love bowed her head theatrically, her gigantic earrings jangling, acknowledging Anna's presence, and the title, together.

The flat was very large, rather strange in arrangement. The bedroom, which Margot and the Great Love shared, opened directly from a vast cavern of a drawing room, with cricked chairs of bulging, faded, dark-pink brocade, tall lamps on taller stands of bronze, patterned rugs and hangings, and prints from Bakst's *Firebird*. In the ceiling was an ornamental fan, and a huge Moroccan birdcage that had no bird in it, yet hung on a chain, door wide open, as if awaiting one.

Beyond the drawing room trailed like a stream a winding corridor. This took in an antiquated bathroom of luminous green-rusted marble, a stuffy study for Margot, something which was a sort of toy room, (where Anna slept), and a little dining chamber with red brocade walls. The corridor ended finally with five funny narrow steps down into a most dismal stone-floored closet, possibly meant as a kitchen, with a thick brown sink and grumbling water tap.

Food was seldom if ever prepared here. Meals were brought from a restaurant across the street, while coffee was ground and Russian tea concocted in the dining room.

The toy room had a slender bed, with white lace curtains. It was almost a doll's bed, but the dolls had been moved from it. Now they sat on a chaise-longue by the wall, all the dolls, seven in number, and two toy animals, a cat upholstered in 'fur' with flame-green eyes, a wooden chicken, intricately carved and painted.

Sometimes all these personalities were carried out and solemnly placed in the drawing room, for an afternoon, or in the dining room for supper. The Great Love saw to this, also to replacing them in their room in seemly attitudes.

To Anna she remarked, "You think the old lady is crazy, yes? You think I have my dolls for babies, because I never get babies?" While the Great Love was saying this, Peepy, (Margot), stood across from them, stiff with unease, glancing at Anna over and over. But the Great Love only concluded, bleakly, "What are children? They tear you open and then ruin your life. And then they grow to men and women and leave you. But these dolls are my friends. My youth, when I was girl, like you."

Anna nodded sympathetically. She saw nothing wrong, not even substitutional, in the dolls, the cat and chicken. They quite charmed her, well-groomed and attractive, demanding nothing.

Margot approached Anna presently.

"I'm so sorry. She forgets things. She's so - not selfish - but wrapped up in her own body, her past. She's kind, really. But she forgot."

"Oh, I don't mind," said Anna airily. She didn't, not at all. What had been said to her at the hospital in Preguna seemed to have nothing to do with her, someone else's news. She had never thought of it, before, and now it was as if the doctor first, and currently Margot, expected her to take seriously to heart something only read of, once or twice, in books.

"Shall I keep the dolls out of your room?"

"It isn't *my* room, Margot. It's your room. It's a lovely room. I like her dolls."

"Just as long as you're quite comfortable."

Anna said she was.

She was.

They let her live among them, both these women. They shared meals with her, very good meals, every day, the sort she and Árpád would have indulged in once a week, perhaps, or less. And they played cards with her, Margot patient and the Great Love cursing her and laughing, and pouring her tiny goblets of Kirsch, giving her spoonfuls of rose-petal jam. They lent her novels and volumes of poetry. Margot took her for walks in the gardens across the street, and glanced at her so repeatedly, worriedly, when children were playing on the grass, or by the fountain.

Her washing was done for her. Margot had even brought three dresses and some underthings from the shop. And shoes. And other items she would need.

Everything in the hospital had been arranged by

Margot. Margot had lied and possibly given bribes. She had said to them all that Anna was her niece, that Anna had a fiancé in France. That Anna was called Annette.

Margot had brought flowers and fruit and chocolates, and once a dish of cabbage dumplings. She had sat with Anna. Indeed Margot was the first person, as the last, Anna saw, opening her eyes again out of the long sleep she began in the chair at the dress-shop.

There had been appalling dreams.

Margot said, as if apologizing for these, "I'm so sorry, *sorry.*"

But Anna felt not unwell, although painfully sore. She wondered, bewildered, if she had been run over by a tram.

"Where is Árpád?" she asked Margot.

But she had never told Margot, or anyone, about Árpád, so it was not extraordinary Margot did not apparently follow her. Then Margot said, sternly, "You mustn't say anything to the doctors. Can you remember, Anna? It will only lead to trouble."

"Do you mean don't speak at all?"

"No. I mean don't say a word to them about - who is it you said?"

"Árpád."

"This man. Oh Anna."

Anna felt wash in towards her, like a returning tide that could not be halted, some dreadful immanence. Not even memory, *knowledge.*

"It was in some of the papers," said Margot. "Even before that, at once, it was quite obvious to me. What you must have done, and why. He nearly killed you, Anna, you were only defending your life. But it's much too dangerous to speak of. Don't tell them anything. They think you're my niece and went dancing at the carnival, and drank a little too much, and then you were sleep-walking - which you had been used to do, but which hadn't happened since you were a child - and you fell down the stairs at my flat."

"But..." said Anna. She closed her eyes.

Margot said, "That was how you bruised your face and cut your mouth, you see. On the stone floor. And the bottom step hurt your stomach. And it was all this that caused the haemorrhage. Naturally I said I was with you, and I brought you here, of course."

Anna said, "I killed him. Did I?"

"*Hush*, Anna. Don't say this now. I saw there was all the other blood. And you'd cut your hand on the knife. But no one else bothered with it. I've lied for you, Anna, to keep you safe. You mustn't speak."

The tears ran slowly, hurting her as the welling blood had hurt.

That evening, when Margot was gone, the doctor questioned Anna. But Margot had told Anna everything she was to say, and where she must be vague and confused, and want her fiancé, the man in France, who had promised to marry her, and give her a beautiful diamond ring.

In the papers, Margot had said, people reportedly had seen a young woman with a badly bruised face, her white breast and white evening gown covered in blood, wandering.

But Margot had insisted that Anna was her relative. Somehow Margot had patched things up, with lies and money. Or no one cared enough, perhaps. Árpád was nothing to them. No one really knew who he was. A disfigured grotesque. A freak.

In an hour or so, another doctor entered and told Anna that she had lost her child, and would never be able to conceive another. They had saved her life. That had been the most urgent task. One could not perform two miracles at once.

She had been with so many men. Never to her knowledge had she been pregnant. She never thought about it. But Árpád had put into her his child, and she hadn't known.

All these messages, warnings and foretellings were only stories, like something overheard on a train.

She lied because Margot had wanted it so badly, and Anna was used to liars, to abetting and assuaging liars.

When she thought of Árpád she cried. Or, the tears simply ran from her eyes. But then she would start to think of something else. And the tears would dry.

After a while, Margot took Anna to the flat. Anna was polite and grateful.

As the car went along the roads, Anna saw the sunlight glimmering on Preguna. She smiled. She wasn't even upset. Grief - was this grief? - so easy.

There must have been embattlement and then truce, between them, Margot and the Great Love.

Margot treated Anna always - as a niece. Demonstrating by every nuance and gesture that she was fond of Anna but nothing else, did not desire anything but to be kind.

And the Great Love, whose volcanic tirade must surely have cracked plaster off the walls, broken glass, filled the air with a laval burning, now acted out this performance of impartial mildness, looking on, intending only to be generous, and noble.

Every move the Great Love made was redolent of

Killing Violets (Gods' Dogs)

these things. A symmetry informed even her rustling breath when she smoked her swarthy cigarettes. She tossed her head and her earrings clashed like a tocsin, but she smiled at Anna, and at Margot. She would be just. She would think no evil, nor speak none.

When she cursed or reviled Anna, at cards or elsewhere, it was *lovingly. Affectionate*, she was not jealous. She said to Anna over and over, sometimes even in words, *You are so young. I have no quarrel with you about this. God is to blame. We are friends.*

And Margot did not touch Anna. She was comradely. If Anna came from the bath in her robe - the embroidered robe Margot had loaned her - Margot's eyes slid over her, as if over some nice article without meaning.

And the Great Love didn't even *watch*. No. She turned her huge eyes away; *I? Not trust you? What nonsense.*

Outside the flat, summer would not end, as if the seasonal needle had stuck in a groove. On and on. The sun-lit days, the dusty dusks, the nights of blurred stars.

Anna said, now and then, that she could now go. She could effortlessly regain her old room. It would be simple to find work.

No - oh no, they clamoured. They vied with each other to keep her there, the symbol of fiery gold by which they knew they had each been virtuous, and would never doubt each other.

Sometimes the Great Love rested in the afternoons, when Margot was at the shop. Anna, instructed also to rest on her white bed, always had.

About three, Anna got up. She went softly and listened through a door to the deep raspy breathing of the

163

Great Love, asleep.

Anna had put a few things into her bag. She wore one of the dresses and a light coat and some shoes, and the little bell-shaped hat Margot had obtained. It no longer hurt Anna to walk. But her stomach felt so light. Like a balloon on a string. Her sense of gravity was affected. Occasionally she paused, and leaned against a wall of the apartment.

Margot's cash was kept in a drawer of the study, very unwisely, the Great Love had always told her so.

Anna stole some of the money. Not very much. It was a horrible thing to do. She wished she hadn't had to, but she had nothing of her own at all.

She wrote a note to Margot, but then tore it up. Anna left the pieces, the bits of words that mentioned sadness and regret and thanks, left them lying in the drawing room on a table.

The birdcage lilted, beckoning the bird. But no bird would come. And the bladed fan, not turning, was as grisly as a guillotine.

Outside, alone, on the hot street of a dying summer that would not admit its death, Anna felt faint as a spectre.

But she made her journey across Preguna to a station, and here she found a train. Margot's thieved cash facilitated a seat, which bore Anna successfully away.

Sitting there in the train, as it churned towards the border, Anna and her lightness, her absence of all centre, seemed tossed in the air, a vile levitation.

Before her lay a year of passage, quite like others she had known, yet different. She was the rain; she came, apocryphal, among the European cities, and in Prague, she beheld the clock with statues, and could not see it, only the rain she had brought with her, dropping down so sadly, from her eyes.

For, without the sorcerous protection of Margot and the Great Love, Anna was beset by winged demons of mystery and dislocation. And by the internal prison of loss.

Such agony was hard as iron, obdurate. She would have feared and fled it, if she had known.

But by that time, it was too late.

In a continent blacker than night, nightmared with beating pinions, she meandered. Like splinters of a mirror, some lights, some segmented scenes, coming and going, she and they, and everything.

Europe was so cold in winter. (Cellars, damp, snow, steel winds.)

And in spring, Europe was a hyacinth, her cities towered with blue. (Men. Flight. Men.)

At last there was a city and a river, and everything had gone. Wandering on the shore, she had a dream of food. Her willingness was to do or become anything, if only she might eat.

This tyranny of her flesh. She had denied her body. It had wanted other things to fill it up. Love. The child. Delight.

Instead she had already made up her mind to sell herself for one meal, gorging and slavering, cramming the void within, (where once her womb had waited like a rose, now withered hard and small), until she had made herself sick.

Chapter Nine: The Tea Ceremony

"Bet you know," said Lilith throatily, "someone that can make me a star."

She had said this as they lay spent in the grass of the Basulte park. And now later, again, in the room of three narrow beds, the third of which was empty.

They were drunk on ginny lemonade, and the sabbat. They had crawled under their separate covers, shivering with weariness, and spite.

"Yes," said Anna. "I do know someone who might."

This was too sweeping, she thought. She added, lying lightly, "He's only in the offices, but he knows people. Oh, he'll like you."

"Never mind that. Will he do me good?"

"I'm sure he will, Lily. You can twist him round your finger."

"Or," said Lilith Izzard, "we could go to Paris. That'd be better."

"Mm, yes," said Anna. "But London first. London's best."

She imagined, going to Paris with Lilith, Lilith clinging to her like an envenomed vine, demanding, bullying, pinching, mocking, teasing, playing unpleasant jokes. And then, when nothing 'good' came of it, no sleek producer in a shining car, to coil Lily in mink and pearls, then Lily turning on her, yellow eyes blazing with vitriol.

"They uz their old tea tumorra."

"What?"

"*Them.*" She meant the Basultes, the Family. "They

166

has it all agether."

Anna recalled, Raoul, the Basulte men, didn't usually join in the feminine tea-times.

"They do it once a month," said Lilith. She yawned, viciously. "Some old tradition of the granddad. All of them. In the saloon. They don't call any of us back, serve themselves, toast buns on the fire, gollocky daft things, like kits. Be ready just after four, and we'll slip off. I'll have the car by the gate."

Oh Christ. The car. The gate.

"Mm," said Anna, sleepily, heart racing.

"That Raoul, though," murmured Lilith, "he's going to be that angry. Both of us, gone."

Anna lay listening to Lilith sleep.

He had said, only tonight, *I won't let you go. I'd kill you.*

Fury moved in her, very deep, a shark in shadows of water.

Why had she come here? Why had she gone anywhere?

She seemed to drift, anchorless and unable to steer, on endless ocean empty of land.

There had been mirages. But no one signalled to her, or answered her cries - her *whispers.* And she also, had none to answer to.

Down in Hell, the kitchen, they used a special kettle for the monthly tea. And into it went the water, and then came one of the footmen, chosen perhaps by lot, grinning and bursting, voluminously to piss.

"It'll do 'em good, that."

The iced cakes would be full of raisins and squashed flies. The great cakes had been cursed, as ever. Bread and butter and God knew what.

When the teapot stood ready, Anna said to the cook, "Can I have my turn?"

"You do, girl," said Mrs Ox.

And the kitchen watched as Anna took off the teapot's bone china lid, put her hands on the rim, and gathered herself and spat deep down among the carefully selected teas and boiling, urinated water.

A few of the maids laughed. This was nothing so enormous.

Shielded by her body, and her curved hand, the small bottle had let go two thirds of its contents. But they hadn't seen. At least, none of them commented upon it. And now the bottle was slipped back into the pocket of her blue, lace-trimmed apron. She had managed to restopper it, too. There was one third left.

All across Europe, Anna had kept the medicine bottle. In case, as Árpád had said, she too 'couldn't go on with it.' She had sat with the bottle sometimes, considering, if she was ready to die yet. No reply came to her. So, she kept it anyway. She had paid for the bottle, after all. Hadn't she?

Only a small teaspoon was necessary - there was much more than that in the teapot. And some left over, too.

A footman and two maids went away with the ritual tea.

For these brief moments Anna was greater than all of them, godlike, knowing this thing which only she could know.

It was raining.

Anna sat in a corner of the kitchen, on a wooden

chair, like the waif in the story, Cinderella. She wondered what she really felt. The godlike cognisance had evaporated.

How long would it take them to die, the six Basultes? (The mouse had curled up happily in its straw.) But this dose was so much stronger, perhaps.

The maids and footmen had returned about ten minutes ago. They did not ever wait on this tea. They had nothing to report.

Suppose Raoul after all had not gone in?

Anna thought of the rain streaming round the orangery beyond the salon, and hissing in the fire, if the fire was alight - which it must be, so that they could toast the buns and bread, as Lilith described.

A clock ticked. Had she ever noticed it before?

Anna had shortened her black dress, this morning. Lilith had advised this. Lilith said she had found other dresses, apparently the ones Raoul gave to Anna in Europe. But Anna herself had no proper shoes, no coat, no hat. Lilith offered Anna nothing at all, except their excursion.

Anna's bag sat on the floor under the wooden chair. She had taken off the apron, with the poison bottle one third full in its pocket, and put the whole thing into the bag.

She was ready. Ready to go. To go on.

Anna thought of Árpád. The last time she had seen him had been in the seconds when he came at her like the tram, his face smeared with lipstick like the dye of the birthmark running. Somehow she hadn't seen him after that.

She never cried now. She looked at memory only for a moment. Then she looked outward, round at the faces of the English servants.

The light was grey and gleaming, fractured by rain and fire, and the electric bulbs, which sometimes stuttered down here, winking in bursts, then settling. These sly pasty faces, with their fat lips and thin lips, and little polished eyes.

Disgusting, they had been made disgusting. And they hung, these people, these *things*, from the Basultes, like pendulous growths on a strong stupid stone wall.

More than escape Raoul Basulte and the Family, more than evade the pack of the servants, Anna decided she had mostly wished to pull down the wall, and let these parasitic victims tumble free. With the wall gone there would be nothing to hold them or clutch on to. They would slither and drop back into their pit. Yes, that was what she wished.

To stop this mutual dependency of filth and dearth, that had changed them all, masters, slaves, to vermin.

Anna got up. No one paid any attention. They had usually let her come and go as she wanted, within the house, letting her run about in the trap.

She went up the stair to the big door, and through into the Smoking Room. She crossed into the corridor, arrived outside the salon.

How silent. No teacups, voices, talk, laughter, swearing. Had it happened?

Anna's hand, on the handle of the door.

If they were alive, she would bob, and say, did they require anything? It was perfectly simple.

But she did not knock.

The door undid the salon and Anna walked inside.

Really, it wasn't such a large room. And the green was almost black, because they had not put on the lamps, or these had for some reason gone out.

The fire burned low. There was a cake lying in the hearth. An iced cake, one of the ones with flies. Just the cake, and the utter density of the silence.

Anna breathed. She saw them, as if they had not been there the instant before, and now they emerged, coming up from underwater.

They had all fallen asleep. They sat in the sage armchairs, leaning back, their hands limp on saucers, plates, all their faces exactly alike as they had always been alike, far too much so.

Only the woman with the lifted face, Raoul's Mother, had let go her cup, and the dregs of her tea had run over the skirt of her white afternoon dress. And Tommy, the man who was the husband of Margaret Lilian, the Basulte with the scar in his eyebrow, he must have been standing up, for he had fallen right over on the carpet. But his face, turned sideways, was completely calm, nearly smiling.

Raoul, she identified him after William, had his mouth slightly open. Maybe he had been in the middle of speaking. He did look a little surprised, as if death had tapped him on the shoulder in mid sentence, making him jump. But not very much.

William - yes it was William - was smiling too, and Margaret Lilian's face had sunk into her smile, like interrupted dough half-risen. Raoul's Father leaned his head on his hand. He had just put out a cigarette, but not quite firmly enough, and a transparent wisp of smoke still twisted from it.

Anna walked over to the teapot. It had been emptied once, and refilled from the silver hot water pot. No one had had time, however, for a second cup of tea.

She stood, in the middle of the peculiar room,

wishing that she could feel more. It was shoddy of her to react so inadequately to this quite monumental scene.

For she had murdered them, successfully. She should rail against them, or beg their pardon, suffused with glory and blame.

But something made her only lift the Mother's teacup from her skirt, and dab with a napkin a crumb off the maroon lips of Lilian, and straighten William's tie. Tidying for the ones who would come later, in an hour or so, and find them.

Anna couldn't remember, even now, the way out through the front of the house. But that didn't create a problem, actually. She went from the salon, shutting the door, and into the red dining-room. One of the long windows opened without difficulty. She stepped out, her bag under her arm, (and oddly, the Mother's bone china cup, painted with birds, in her right hand) hatless, coatless, to the terrace and the veil of the cold summer rain.

Lilith drove erratically, but the car kept moving, like a wonder. Lilith chattered. She was excited, and a little tiddly, for she had stolen more gin from her mother's pub, and they passed the bottle between them.

The car had been waiting at the gateway, as stipulated.

"You were a time," had said Lilith.

Soaked through, Anna got into the car. She had stowed by then the teacup in her bag.

Initially the car wouldn't start again. Then it did.

"Know the way? Of course I do."

Miraculously, Lilith had thieved a map from her father, (men made roads, women dispensed beverages.)

Lilith could read the map - yet also she seemed homing in on the capital, unstoppable. Anna never doubted her.

Trees in rain poured close about them, and sometimes broke apart on the blank tundra of a reaped field.

They did not pass the village. They seemed to pass nothing, other than trees and fields, and now and then some saturated black shed, or a cottage squashed back from the road in clumps of briars or apple trees, perhaps with a wet dog barking on a chain.

Then the day turned, a sort of limbo of partial darkness began, greenish dusk that did not lessen or increase.

In this, an occasional light now aqueously splashed, spilled down the windows and away.

Lilith told Anna many things. All her (eventless) life. Her dreams. How wild this was. What she expected Anna to do for her and produce for her, like a good fairy, out of thin air.

Anna listened placidly, and shared the gin.

Sometimes there were distant churches. They reminded Anna, for a reason she could not fathom, of lighthouses.

Darkness did come eventually, evolving like a new element, finding its way uncertainly at first, and then with total confidence.

In the dark there was nothing but night and rain, and lights like arrows now, fired right by them, or possibly at them, and missing.

Lilith stopped the car.

"Have to make a visit," said Lilith.

Anna mystified, still benign.

"You *know*," said Lilith primly. "It's a long journey,

this. I've drunk too much. Better not have any more."

A fox, she got out of the car. She wore the green Paris dress, and a smart mackintosh Raoul had bought Anna. Lilith's head was tied in a lurid scarf with two holes and one frayed end. But she was a fox, anyway.

The fox took herself into the rain-gusting bushes by the side of the road. The curtains of rain closed her behind them.

Anna put the gin bottle to one side, and opened her bag quietly. Presently she glanced at her own face in the hand-mirror they had left her. There she was. Anna Moll. Pale in darkness, curiously incomplete. It seemed to her that a feature had been rubbed out from her face. The nose, was it? Or the lips. Not, definitely not, the eyes, which had been filled up by the pupil, and become black.

Then Lilith returned from the bushes, glittering in headlamps and water.

Her eyes belonged to a witch. She was demon, fox, creature.

"Onna Lonun. Only a few miles. I seen them posts."

I must try to understand her. Keep hold until we get there.

The car was persuaded again to start, and they drove on, through the tunnel of the dark. And soon, soon, there began, like the product of some scene-shifter's art, to be streets, and short stacks of brick villas, and new masses of blinking spear-cast lights.

"Is it far?" Anna, softly.

"Not far. Where do we have to go to get with your friend?"

"Oh, he's got a wonderful apartment near..." Anna tensed her mind, "near the Houses of Parliament - near the river. A huge drawing room, and a room full of dolls."

Lilith sneered. A man with a room of dolls.

Anna explained the dolls were valuable. They had come from Russia before the great revolution which deposed the Czar.

"Worth a bit," said Lilith.

"Oh, yes."

Lilith began again to fantasise aloud about her famous fate. She was going to rule the world.

Anna was so cold. Her soaked dress hadn't quite dried to her body. She felt feverish and lax. Inside all this, her brain ticked heavily like the kitchen clock.

She saw it was a city now. Even the rain was thinner, and catching the lights, sparkled.

Spidery buildings craned to a purple sky. And there - was that a river?

It was late, no one about. (Had they ever stopped for petrol? Had Lilith seen to it?) Things had rolled from Anna's mind, but that didn't matter.

There was only one more thing to do.

"Stop over there."

"Pull over? What for?"

"Just to get my bearings. Look, there's a pub there. We can go in and ask."

Lilith grunted gracelessly. She pushed the fanfare scarf off her head. She drove into the side street, a sort of alley, with rotten walls rising up from it, and a lamp chilled blue, and the rain like sapphires...

"You go in that pub, Annie. Um nod gumma do it."

Annie, Lilith's slave. Her bitch dog.

"Of course I will, Lily. Oh Lily," as the car pulled up with a deadly ending squeal, "we've done it. You're so clever. And you're going to be a queen. Let's just have a taste of the gin."

"Uv had anuff."

"No, you must. To toast your future. Look, Lily. I brought one of their cups. I stole it. You mustn't drink from the bottle, m'lady. You're going to be a queen."

Lilith's face, stretched tight with unknowledge and disdain, bloomed in a foul, condescending little smile.

"A wull thun."

And Anna drenched into the teacup painted with birds, the gin, which she had topped up with poison as Lilith made water in the rain.

Lilith did not even notice Anna didn't drink. Anna was a bit-player, the Heroine's servitor.

"Here's to you, dearie," said Anna. "All the best."

And Lilith put the cup to her lips, and drank down all the gin.

Meaning To Continue

That was a strange day. Anyone might have thought so. The rain had stopped, and there had been a week of sunshine, and the city became, somehow, even more bizarre, threatening, in the heat, and the long dry evenings when the sun refused to go down beyond the sooty buildings. The birds here flew round and round, chirruping, as if they were insane. And this day concluded in a sunset that seemed never likely to stop, carmine and peach, and people were standing on the streets or hesitating getting off the buses; coming to windows; pointing, staring at the sunset, as if they had never seen such colours. As if never before had any day come to an end.

In the morning, she had tried to sell the diamond ring.

Until then, it hadn't seemed absolutely necessary. From Lilith, Anna had taken clothes, the dress and raincoat, and also the money Lilith had brought with her in a cheap purse. Had she stolen the money, with the gin and the map, and, presumably, the car? Or was it only Anna's money anyway, stolen originally by the servants.

Anna took a room in a small musty hotel. They gave you breakfast, unappealing English fare, burnt meats and fish and broken eggs, fried, and great slabs of bread with yellow grease spread on them. And stodgy dark brown tea.

For a couple of days Anna bought fruit in a market, and ate it at night in her room, which was, according to a notice on the wall, forbidden.

There were men, too. You found them mostly in the pubs. They bought you a drink or two, and then came a stumbling up dim stairs or even into a hotel room just like Anna's own. They would say, "Five shillings all right?" Or even take her for a meagre supper, and that was it.

She kept thinking she must not stay in London. It was in fact a fearful place. And although she had found the river, with rusty ships rubbing their sides on its banks, it did not seem to her to be the river she had heard and read of. But there was a huge clock. It presided over the mud-flats and the warehouses. Along the concrete shore shone street-lamps. The buses were papered over with advertisements and injunctions. So many things, showing you, telling you, what to do, what not to do.

Anna knew she must find a way to leave. It had always been like this, the compulsion, the impetus, to volition, progressing or escaping.

Somehow she had saved the ring. And then she went to a shop, which was pointed out to her, and inside, in the same sort of fudge-dark she recalled when Raoul had bought it, she offered the ring up.

She felt no wrench, in doing this. She had only to wrench a little in getting it off. But she had lost weight, or attachment, it had not been impossible to slough the ring, as in the house it had.

There was an old man behind the grill. "Let me see."

The ring was pushed under the grill. The old man abruptly malignantly laughed. "This? What do you take me for? It's glass."

The lizard woman in the village pub had said exactly this.

Anna was prepared.

"Can you give me anything?"

"The time of day, my dear."

He was a Jew. She recollected how Jews were hated. She noted, conceivably, why.

He passed her back the glass diamond, chuckling, and she foresaw he would tell everyone he had contact with his colossal joke, the young slut who had come in and tried to get money on such rubbish.

After this episode, she sat on a seat under a dispirited tree. She sat there most of the day.

Three days ago she had no longer had any money to pay for the room. So she had left the hotel without settling her bill.

Now all the money was gone. And she was so hungry. Ridiculously hungry, for even this morning she had bought herself some toast and a pot of tea at a café.

Through the late afternoon she walked about. Sometimes men looked at her, and once one looked right at her, and she smiled, but then he seemed afraid and hurried on.

She went through an arid park, where the trees had metal leaves, and flowers bloomed with a parched red scent.

Children were feeding the blue pigeons.

Anna stared at this. She could taste the chunks of stale bread in her mouth. The pond gleamed, making her thirsty for gin and bitters. But also she had a curious notion, picking up a child, and licking its face, delicately. What would it taste of? It would laugh, and so would she.

There was a boat-train from some station she had heard of, (with Raoul?), and this would take her over to France. France would be better.

She needed to meet a man who was going to France.

Why was it a strange day, really? It wasn't so strange. Even the sunset, pomegranates and peaches, and all these people staring at it. Forbidden fruit.

At last, the dark closed the sky, and lamps were lighting up as if at the touch of phantoms.

The big clock boomed. How many strokes? Was it seven?

Anna gazed down on to the iron surface of the river. She had returned to it, vainly searching for something. Items were thrown into canals and rivers.

But the hot evening made her slow. She leaned on the wall above the water, and she could smell food from some restaurant, and all at once she didn't want it so much. It wasn't really so important, to eat. Or to do anything.

Could it be, she wondered, if London was after all the last of the cities, her destination, its parched vistas so redolent of terminus, like a station itself, where trains would enter, but from which no passengers went away.

The man stood under the lamp, lighting a cigarette.

He was tall, slimly built, well-dressed. His hat was tilted a little, and his hair was very fair. He was not like Raoul.

She knew he had been looking at her, almost intently, and now, seeing her look up in turn, he walked without haste across the pavement.

"Good evening. Did you see the sunset?"

"Oh... yes."

"It was very beautiful."

"Yes."

He smiled. "I think you're a foreigner, like myself."

Had he said this? Raoul had once said this, but the man was not like Raoul.

"Are you?" she asked.

"A foreigner? To London, yes." He took out a packet of cigarettes and offered them to her. When she accepted one, he lit it for her. And as he leaned closer, she saw, under his right eye, a small birthmark, only the faintest of colours, only the size of an English farthing.

Her heart beat once, shaking her. For a moment the city pulsed out, but then came back, complete and steady, as if nothing whatsoever had happened.

"Perhaps," he said, "you'll let me take you somewhere."

Anna said, "Yes, of course. But I'm afraid I need money rather badly."

"I thought that you might. Let's go somewhere for a quiet drink. That's what they say here, you know. A quiet drink. Not a noisy one. I'm sure we can come to an agreement."

A weight lifted away from Anna. This man would be her salvation. But as the weight dispersed, she sensed how it had held her to the earth. Now she was in the air, with nothing to hold on to.

He offered his arm, then. When he did this, deep pain stirred inside her. But it was only memory. What she was accustomed to. It was of no importance, the slight mark on his face beneath the dark blue eye. It had not marred him or driven him into the wilderness.

She took his arm, and he was real and ordinary. They walked at an even pace over the burned cracked paving, and up a hill, and there was a public house with a curious sign, not a dragon, but a headless woman, holding her head up in one hand.

He glanced at this. His mouth was wry. "They have an odd way of looking at things, the English."

Inside, the smoke had made a mist. There was the odour of beer and spirits, sawdust, and a tinge of vomit and disinfectant.

She went into a booth, a high fence of wood, and sat at a wooden table almost black, scarred with cigarettes and ringed by past glasses.

He brought her a present glass of gin, very strong, three or four measures, and also with something sweet in it she didn't really like. And some sandwiches, coarsely cut, on a plate.

"Their beef is good," he said. "Eat something."

She ate a mouthful or two. But her hunger had gone. It had no longer seemed necessary to be hungry.

She drank about half the gin, and parts of her rose and left her. She felt relaxed now, and sad without urgence.

"My name is Virág," he said. "May I call you Anna?"

She must have told him her name, she always did. They tended to ask, liking to have a label for you. And sometimes you got one back, "Call me George, Arthur, Bertie." Or it was, "I won't give my name. Don't mind, do you?"

Virág. Oh, not an English name. She would have liked better a French name.

They smoked two more cigarettes.

"You see," she said, "I find I need to cross the Channel."

"1 understand. Don't, worry, Anna. Maybe we'll go together. Would you object to that?"

Her heart tried to fly up with relief, but could not summon the energy. And she was already adrift in the air.

"No. Not at all."

"We may need to go somewhere first. That would be all right, wouldn't it?"

She smiled. Her smile felt tired and stiff. She must be cautious. Not put him off. This was so lucky.

"Let's talk a while," he said. "The streets are so crowded now. In an hour or so it will be easy to find a taxi."

(He was not like Raoul.) He was not like Árpád. She had been terrified that he was, and longed for that, and now her disappointment engulfed her.

She had not said good-bye to him. She hadn't looked for him. She had left him lying on the floor of the room, untidily, with the ripped curtain blowing. It seemed like yesterday.

This man - Virág - had asked her something.

"I'm sorry. What did you say?"

"Have you been in London long?"

"Oh. No. Only a few days."

"It's a bad city. Unfriendly."

"Yes, I think so."

"But you were somewhere else before?"

He was offering her another cigarette. She took it. "In the countryside."

"How interesting," he said. "But it's been wet."

"Yes, it rained."

"They don't like foreigners here," he said, "especially in the country. Don't you find?"

She said nothing.

The man - Virág - said, "Were you working somewhere?"

"I was in a house. A friend's house."

"That must have been interesting," he said.

"Not really. He wasn't truly a friend to me."

Virág's lips curled into his smile. "The villain. Did you run away?"

"Yes. I ran away."

"I'm surprised he let you go."

"Oh - he didn't stop me."

"Didn't he?"

"No. "

"I'd have thought," said Virág, "he'd have tried to make you stay. Just for another night. What a wretch. An Englishman, of course."

"Yes."

"Perhaps you had some difficulty with his family. They're prudish, here. Don't you find that?"

"I didn't find that, no."

"And they treat their servants badly." Anna had finished her drink. He took the glass. "We'll have another. The streets will be less crowded soon."

He went with their glasses back towards the bar.

The room had filled up inside its fulvous haze of smokes and fumes. In the corner, some old men were playing a game of some sort on the table. And a crone was going about with a basket of mauve flowers.

Anna had an urge to get up and walk out of the pub that was a headless woman, while Virág was busy buying her another drink. It would be straightforward, surely.

But she couldn't be bothered really. It was all right. So she sat where she was, and the cigarette burned down in her fingers.

When he returned, he put the full glass before her, and pushed the plate of uneaten sandwiches aside.

She saw he was quite handsome. His eyes were clear

and intense. His mouth was classically shaped, and his hands. As a lover, he might be exciting. His smile was kind, yes, kind, and thoughtful. When his fingers brushed hers, she sensed that he took great care with her.

All this augured well. But she was tired now. The drink made her tired.

The old woman with the flowers came up to their table.

"Violets for your young lady?"

There was a tired face. To be so old. All those years of living, on and on, without remit. One could never grow old. The old were another species.

"Here," he said. He gave the woman - Anna saw - a note of money. "Would you like some violets? Forced, I'd imagine."

She thought of Árpád, the flowers in the bowls, the dorisa. Did they force violets here?

Her eyes filled with tears. They were tears of tiredness.

Then he had leant across, was pinning the violets on the mackintosh collar, for she had worn the mackintosh even in the summer evening.

She smelled the perfume of the violets, like confectionery almost, mixed with the aroma of moist earth and shadows. But then they had no scent after all. She had only somehow conjured it.

The woman was saying God would bless the man, Virág. Something like that.

She went straight to the bar and regally ordered stout.

Anna saw the flower-basket put on the floor, knocked against, of less importance now. One tear ran down her face. How tired she must be. Yes, she was, she was.

"Gin," she said, "makes a woman cry, doesn't it."

"Does it?"

"They say so, here. Lilian said so. Or Lilith said so."

"Lilian," he said, consideringly, "Lilith. Are they the same?"

(She wondered when he would take her away, to his room. Soon, she hoped. She wanted to sleep.)

"They were women at the house of your friend?" he added.

"...Yes."

"Perhaps they came up to London with you."

"No. Why would they?"

"Oh, everyone in the country wants to come to the city. The people in the cities want to get out into the country."

Anna's head drooped. For a second she was asleep. Then the jerk of her neck brought her awake again, violently almost, and she was alert.

"You've dropped your cigarette." He offered her the packet.

"No, thank you. I wonder..." she hesitated, placatory, "is there somewhere we could go? I haven't been sleeping well, you see. If I could just sleep for an hour."

"Men always like to look after you, don't they, Anna," he said. "Or use you. I knew a girl like that. She had this quality. You had to stop yourself putting your arm around her, protecting her. You wanted to take her to bed. It was difficult to resist, because she didn't resist. Probably someone - your friend - brought you to England. What were the terms?"

"Terms..." she said.

"He wanted to go on sleeping with you, but you

were to have a job in the house. Learn a maid's work, something like that. And then he'd give you a magnificent reference, and you could find a good job in London."

"No, it wasn't that," said Anna vaguely. "He wanted to marry me."

"Did he? Are you sure, Anna? Perhaps you're confused. Or I must have heard the story wrongly. He just wanted the use of you, I thought, and his payment was pretty mean. This false reference, and some clothes, some costume jewellery. But then. You were safer out of Europe."

Anna leaned back and her head rested on the smooth wood of the booth. She saw the man - Virág - from a considerable distance. She reached down the miles for her glass, and drank the gin with the sweet thing in it.

"The girl I knew," said the man, "something like that happened to her." He nodded, attentively. His eyes were quite pure, not cruel or deadly at all. He had sorrowful eyes, like a saint in an icon. He put his hand over her hand, and his clasp was warm, it was a reassurance. He said, "Have you seen the papers?"

"What papers - do you mean my passport?"

He said, in French, "I mean the journals. The news."

She shook her head, the smooth back of the booth helping her.

Virág - the man - said, "They found a young girl in a car in a side street. She was naked but for some underclothes. She'd been given poison, a strychnine derivative, probably. An odd thing. She'd come from a house in the country, a country family, and they too, Anna, were found dead, sitting round their teapot."

Anna sighed. She withdrew her hand and put it to

the forced violets on her collar, stroking them softly. Someone had told her, they only lasted a day. She should have taken them somewhere happy, to a theatre, in her hair, then set them in a glass which had held Champagne, to dream away the night into death.

"It began in Preguna," he said. "Are you familiar with Preguna? A quaint place. They have a carnival." He was a policeman. She had seemed to know it for some while. "There was a woman who lied for you, Anna, but no one was entirely satisfied. You killed him although you loved him, didn't you, since you were in fear of your life. They might have saved you, Anna, then. But now look what you've done. Do you say you went mad in Preguna, Anna? Is that it?"

She looked away from him. His face was cool with sorrow, and he had told her, he wanted to hold her, shield her from it all.

"Poor little Anna. I don't think you're quite mad. Perhaps they will think so. Let's hope they will."

"Thank you for the drink," she said. "And the violets. When we get there, will they let me put them in water? They're thirsty, I can tell."

"Yes, Anna. It will be all right."

"I'm ready now," she said.

He frowned. "Are you? You're stronger stuff than I am. I kept hoping you wouldn't look up, by the river. And then I thought you might give me the slip."

She smiled, a little. "I'm too tired."

She thought that was it, the answer. She was so tired by now. She had done enough. She was prepared to reach the end, and lie down, and sleep for ever.

Anna rose first, and then Virág got up. He offered her his arm, and she was still glad of it, to keep her attached to the world just a minute longer, to what was left of the world.

As they walked from the pub, the old flower-seller had begun to sing. She had a hard confidant voice, cracked like pavement. The stout slopped in her hand, spoiling the forgotten violets in the basket by her feet. But they were already dying. Uprooted, adrift, trapped, pinned, at the mercy of everything, it almost seemed that was what they had come to life for, to die. Since killing them was so easy.

About the Author

 Tanith Lee was born in North London (UK) in 1947. Because her parents were professional dancers (ballroom, Latin American) and had to live where the work was, she attended a number of truly terrible schools, and didn't learn to read – she is also dyslectic – until almost age 8. And then only because her father taught her. This opened the world of books to Lee, and by 9 she was writing. After much better education at a grammar school, Lee went on to work in a library. This was followed by various other jobs – shop assistant, waitress, clerk – plus a year at art college when she was 25-26. In 1974 this mosaic ended when DAW Books of America, under the leadership of Donald A Wollheim, bought and published Lee's *The Birthgrave*, and thereafter 26 of her novels and collections.

Since then Lee has written around 90 books, and approaching 300 short stories. 4 of her radio plays have been broadcast by the BBC; she also wrote 2 episodes (*Sarcophagus* and *Sand*) for the TV series *Blake's 7*. Some of her stories regularly get read on Radio 7.

Lee writes in many styles in and across many genres, including Horror, SF and Fantasy, Historical, Detective, Contemporary-Psychological, Children and Young Adult. Her preoccupation, though, is always people.

In 1992 she married the writer-artist-photographer John Kaiine, her companion since 1987. They live on the Sussex Weald, near the sea, in a house full of books and plants, with two black and white overlords called cats.

CPSIA information can be obtained at www.ICGtesting.com
Printed in the USA
BVOW03s2251130814

362725BV00001B/287/P